MAVERICK

MAVERICK

BILL CRAIG

ABSOLUTELY AMAZING eBOOKS

ABSOLUTELY AMAZING eBOOKS

Published by Whiz Bang LLC, 926 Truman Avenue, Key West, Florida 33040, USA.

Maverick copyright © 2018 by Bill Craig. Electronic compilation/ paperback edition copyright © 2017 by Whiz Bang LLC.

For information contact:
Publisher@AbsolutelyAmazingEbooks.com

ISBN-13: 978-1945772894 (Absolutely Amazing Ebooks)

ISBN-10: 1945772891

MAVERICK

PROLOGUE

The small wagon train had been trudging along day after day through the Kansas territory while the travelers kept looking west. The more miles behind them, the closer to their goal. The covered wagons had crossed on the trails used by farmers to drive their cattle to market. They had seen what they thought were clouds banked on the horizon.

The train stopped for the night and the wagon master told them that tomorrow they would be arriving in the Colorado territory. The next morning, the sun dazzled them as they push on. Suddenly, they realized the cloud bank they thought they saw really was the Rocky Mountains. A very impressive fourteen-thousand foot in height, directly in front of them, a hundred miles or so away. Many were relieved, others jumped for joy. The ladies of the small wagon train put their baking skills together and that night they had a party.

Chapter 1

The sun was directly above his head when he opened his eyes. His mouth was dry and full of dirt as he pushed to his knees. Blinking the dust from his eyes, he looked around in amazement. Burnt former covered wagons lay smoking on the mud caked dirt. Dead slaughtered bodies were everywhere. His head was throbbing and when he touched the spot his hand came away slick with oozing blood.

He remembered a rifle butt to his forehead but not much else. He checked his pockets and they were empty, no wallet, nothing to tell him who he was. Slowly, he searched around, looking for any survivors, checking their belongings for any monies and supplies he stuffed into a saddle bag that had been left behind. He found a pistol, leading him to believe that it had not been Indians that had attacked the wagon train. It appeared he had been the lone survivor of the attack and he had been left for dead.

The Colt Peacemaker .45 was only partially loaded, three rounds having been fired from it. He dug around and found a full box of .45 Colt shells and loaded five chambers, leaving the one beneath the hammer empty. There was a holster that fit the gun and he belted it around his narrow hips. He had also secured a Winchester rifle and a box of shells for it. A still standing barrel of water was used to bathe his head wound and wash the dirt from his face. His final act before he started west was to reach down for an abandoned Stetson hat to cover his wound and protect him from the sun.

According to his reflection in the water, he saw that he was a ruggedly handsome sort, with dark hair and blue eyes, even features and white teeth. He had filled two canteens from the barrel before draping the straps across his shoulders and then he started walking towards the mountains towards what he knew he would eventually reach, a town named Denver City.

~ ~ ~

He was foot sore and bone weary when he trudged into the bustling town. From Denver's start, a few years prior, as a gold and silver mining town through its transformation into a supplier of goods and services was the home of the Denver Pacific Railway along the South Platte River. It had always been a place where miners, workers, and travelers could spend their hard-earned money. Saloons and gambling dens sprung up quickly after the founding. During his time in Denver City, he kept his head down and to himself. He quickly gained some employment with a farrier, shoeing horses, which allowed him to purchase a good horse, worked there for a week and continue on his trek into the high mountains where he aimed to start his own search for gold.

~ ~ ~

A few days later, he arrived at the small mining town of Golden along the banks of Clear Creek River between the foothills of the Rocky Mountains to the west and two mesa's named North and South Tabletop to the east. It was a small boom town bustling with activity and known as the last flat place before rising up into the snow-capped peaks beyond.

The folks milling around regarded him with no small amount of curiosity. He trudged towards a hotel and stepped up on the boardwalk to enter. Several sets of eyes watched him vanish inside.

"Can I help you?" the thin young man behind the desk asked, as he walked up to it.

"I'd like a room," the man said.

"Two bits a day, pay a week in advance," the unfriendly man frowned.

"Fine, I'd like a room for a week," he said.

"Payment is up front," the thin man sniffed disdainfully.

"I expect change," he said, putting a Double Eagle on the counter that he had lifted off one of the dead back at the camp. The clerk's eyes liked to have bugged out of his head at the sight of the twenty-dollar gold piece.

"Yes, Sir!" he snapped, scooping up the coin and dropping it into the cash register and counting back change.

He smiled and said, "Draw me a bath."

"Yes, Sir!" the clerk smiled and asked, "If you would kindly sign the register, please, Sir."

He looked at the big book for a moment. He didn't remember his name, but he remembered what they called unbranded cattle. He reached down and wrote the name Maverick in the register. When the clerk turned the book back to himself, he looked at it quizzically.

"Mister Maverick? No first name?" the clerk asked, looking puzzled.

"Just Maverick," he said. The clerk handed him a key and he headed up the stairs, wondering if some of the men that had attacked the wagon train were in this town.

Groaning, he stripped off his clothing while a young man wheeled in a tub and proceeded to fill it with hot water. Maverick sighed, as he lowered himself into the steaming water, felt his muscles loosening and un-bunching. He ducked his head beneath the water and came up. He took a bar of soap and scrubbed his hair and body and rinsed them good before standing up. He had given the boy money and his sizes and sent him to the little General Store to get him some clothes while his own were being laundered. Once he was dry and the tub had been hauled back out to be emptied and rinsed for the next person, he tucked a chair under the door knob and stretched out on the bed. And went to sleep and started dreaming.

~ ~ ~

He had joined the wagon train not far out of Missouri, hired to serve as out-rider and scout. The wagon master hadn't asked about his past, for which he was grateful. Death seemed to follow him wherever he went. First in Virginia, then Ohio and Kentucky. Someone had tried to kill him again in St. Louis and it was just by chance he had escaped the trap that had been set for him.

They were three days into Kansas when the raiders hit the wagon train, riding out of the night, shooting into the wagons and throwing torches. He had been sleeping beneath a wagon when it had been set fire and had scrambled out, dragging his revolver from the holster and firing, dropping one raider. He heard something behind him and spun, just in time to catch a rifle butt in the face.

~ ~ ~

Maverick snapped awake, his body soaked in the cold sweat of the nightmare. He stood and padded to the window and looked out. Darkness had fallen. His stomach growled, and he remembered it had been some time since he had eaten back in Denver City. He dressed in the dark, still not wanting to announce his awakening to any that might be outside watching.

Somebody wanted him dead and had been about trying to make it happen for a while, if his nightmare was to be believed. It would be nice to know who wanted him dead. Hell, for that matter it would be nice to know who he was. Maverick shook his head.

Perhaps he would try to make a new life with his new name and whoever was after him would believe him dead and left on the Kansas territory plains to rot. However, if they kept coming, he would fight and maybe he could find out who was after him and why.

The saloon was loud and full of people. Maverick sat at a table by himself, sipping on a cold beer. Other patrons eddied and swirled around him but up close, a circle of stillness hung around him. No one approached him on their own and when they did, the invisible circle of quiet that surrounded made them back off.

One of the working girls dropped into the chair across from him. Her hair was golden, and her eyes were blue. She wore a heavy dark green velvet off the shoulder dress with black lace trim. Her golden tresses were pinned up in a bun with a few loose curls dangling down around her face. "You're new in town," she observed.

"I am," Maverick took a sip of his beer.

"I'm May," the girl volunteered.

"Good to be somebody. Nice to meet you, Miss May," Maverick told her.

"You're not much of a talker, are you?" May looked at him.

"Nope," he replied, quietly.

"If you change your mind, just ask for me," May batted her eyes, as she stood up and sashayed away, wiggling her bustle and many petticoats at him. Another time, another place, he might have taken her up on her offer. But this was neither. Not with unknown men who wanted him dead for unknown reasons hunting for him.

No ... caution was his watchword for the time being. Until he found out more about who he was, and why someone wanted him dead. Maverick sipped his cold frothy beer until a waitress arrived with a plate full of steak, potatoes and beans with a side plate of hot cornbread muffins and freshly churned butter.

Maverick wolfed it down and when he had finished sopping of the last of the juices with the last of the corn muffins, he popped it into his mouth with a contented sigh. For the first time in days he was starting to feel kind of human. The piano player was pounding out a lively rendition of *'Red River Valley'* when a new man entered the bar.

He was tall and thin, wiry, with dark skin and a pencil thin mustache below his flat-crowned Stetson. Something about him looked vaguely familiar. Enough so that the man calling himself Maverick slipped the leather hammer thong off his Peacemaker. Maverick pulled down the brim of his hat, letting it keep his face in shadow, as his blue eyes followed the newcomer.

He watched as May approached the man who shoved her roughly away. May made a comment and then spat at him. The cowboy spun around and slapped her, knocking the saloon girl to the ground. Almost before he realized what he was doing, Maverick was on his feet and the Colt in his hand was firing. The cowboy slammed into the wall, blood spreading across the front of his shirt and slid down the wall, leaving a trail of dark red on the hardwood floor.

"I don't like a man who abuses women," Maverick said to nobody in particular, spinning his gun and dropping it back into the holster. May was back on her feet and came to him once more.

"Thank you, Sir. I don't even know your name . . ." she started.

"Maverick," he told her, then he stood and headed for the door.

It was still dark outside except for a few oil lanterns hanging above the street attached to the buildings. Maverick was glad his shirt was dark blue checkered flannel and not a starch white which would stand out in the night and that he had a warm sheepskin coat. He walked back to the hotel. In the morning, he would take his horse and head out up into the Rockies.

~ ~ ~

"Who was that man, May?" May's boss, Ted Willis asked. They hadn't got around to electing a sheriff yet. Not since the last one quit, heading into the Rockies to try his hand at prospecting.

"Which one?" May asked, taking a drink of whiskey to calm her shattered nerves.

"Either of them. Had you seen either one before tonight?"

"No, I hadn't. The one that stood up for me, he said his name was Maverick," May said, taking another sip of whiskey.

"Maverick. What the hell kind of name is that?" Willis wanted to know.

"Why don't you go ask him?" May glared at her boss.

"Uh, no, that's okay," Willis turned abruptly away.

Maverick, or whatever his name was, was a man familiar with using a gun. Ted Willis had no plans whatsoever of getting crosswise of him. Gus, the bouncer, had dragged the body out back and was behind the bar when Willis reached it again.

"Ed Montero, Boss," Gus told him the name on the papers that the man had been carrying. Montero was a half-Mex that was known to be hunting trouble in the area. Originally from down on the Rio Grande, Montero had fled Mexico ahead of the Mexican Federales, and just a jump and a skip ahead of the Texas Rangers.

"Montero was bad news," Willis nodded.

"Not anymore," Gus shrugged.

"No, no, I guess not," Willis sighed. He bit off the end of a fat cigar and lit it. There had been rumors that Montero had hooked up with a gang, but he had seen no sign of it. But if it were true, he wondered if those men would come looking for the Mexican. Puffing on his cigar, Ted Willis poured himself a shot of whiskey.

~ ~ ~

Jonas Wilder had heard the shots from inside the saloon and had stepped to the shadows and waited. He and Montero had ridden in to meet with Bud Riley and let him know what had happened when they had hit the wagon train. The rest of the gang was camped out on the plains in the Indian Territory near the Indian Reservations.

He had watched from the shadows as a well-built man left the saloon and headed down the street towards the hotel. There was something familiar about the way the man moved. Jonas Wilder made a snap decision and decided to follow him to find out who the man was. He had a bad feeling about the man.

~ ~ ~

Maverick kept to the middle of the dusty street when he left the saloon. His Colt was still loose in its holster. The darkness was anything but friendly tonight. He could feel it in his bones. Somewhere behind him, he heard a spur jingle as someone tried to move quietly behind him. He was being followed. Nobody should be following him, which meant they were probably up to no good. Maverick stepped into shadows and vanished. He was folded against the side of a wooden sided building, his Colt in his hand, waiting as the man following him drew closer.

The man trudged past, his eyes searching the darkness for the man that he had been following. Maverick waited and watched, but there were no gas lights close enough to give him a look at the man's face. The man went on and Maverick faded down the alley, paralleling the man's track to the hotel. The man took up a spot where he could observe the front door of the hotel. Maverick nodded to himself and then went around and entered from the back.

Silently, he made his way to his room and slipped a chair under the door knob and moved the bed out of range of both door and window before pulling off his boots and gun belt and slipped down on the bed to sleep. His gun was within easy reach.

Chapter 2

Bud Riley tossed the whore off him when he heard the first shot and reached for his gun. He waited for several long moments, tense and ready, expecting trouble. There were no more shots and he relaxed, slipping his revolver back into the holster and grabbing the whore once more, returning to what he had been doing with a great amount of gusto.

It was a good hour before Bud Riley, dressed once more, made his way down the stairs of the saloon to the main floor and wandered to the bar. He ordered a whiskey and the barkeep filled his glass.

"Anybody asking after me?" Riley asked.

"Nope, but we had us a shooting earlier," Willis shrugged, wiping at the bar with a wet cloth.

"Who got shot?" Riley asked.

"A feller by the name of Montero, a Mex bad man," Willis replied.

"Who done it?" Riley asked, his tone sharper.

"Stranger in town, fella by the name of Maverick," Willis replied.

"What the hell kind of name is that?" Riley asked.

"Hell if I know," Willis shrugged.

"Montero say anything to anybody?" Riley asked.

"Slapped one of my whores when she tried to talk to him, but nobody else," Willis continued polishing down the bar.

"That whore got a name?" Riley asked.

"May, the blonde in the green velvet gown," Willis pointed her out. He watched the man approach her and wondered briefly if there wasn't about to be more trouble. Riley spoke to her briefly and then headed for the door. That surprised him. He walked out from behind the bar and approached May.

"What was that all about?" Willis asked.

"Guy wanted to know about Maverick. There ain't much to tell," May replied.

"Keep it that way," Willis told her. He had a bad feeling about it all.

~ ~ ~

Jonas Wilder stood on the street in the darkness wondering. That feller that had shot Montero had lost him in the shadows and that wasn't something that happened too often. Wilder had a reputation as a manhunter. Now, he had been given the slip in the night by a man who was a stranger in this little one-horse town. Wilder didn't like it. He had never lost a man that he was trailing before. That meant that this guy was better than anyone he had ever seen.

"Looking for me, friend?" A voice asked from the darkness and he felt the cold steel of a gun-barrel at his neck.

"I'm not looking for anybody, friend," Wilder replied. Sarcastically. He was suddenly very afraid.

"I'm afraid I don't believe you. You've been on my back trail since I walked out of the saloon. I take exception to that," the voice said.

"Okay, I just wondered who you were," Wilder shrugged.

"That's a good way to get yourself dead. I might think you're reaching for your gun if it happens again. Then there's going to be a big hole through your chest," the man said.

"Sorry about that, Sir."

"You should be," the voice said, and then Wilder saw stars exploded through his vision.

Maverick watched the man fall to the ground and he holstered his pistol. He didn't bother with the hammer thong, as he stepped back into the shadows and made his way to the hotel. Maverick slipped back inside without being seen. Trouble was riding his back trail. He had tried to sleep but couldn't do it, not while that man waited. Perhaps waiting until morning would be too late. He gathered his things and packed them into saddle bags and slipped out and down the back staircase. Maverick made his way to the livery stable to collect his horse.

The hostler was an old man with a thick white beard and long handles worn beneath suspenders and a pair of brushed canvas pants tucked into knee-high boots. His name was Mossy. He snapped awake as Maverick entered the stables.

"That's a good horse with a lot of bottom in him," Mossy told him.

"He is. A strawberry roan with more bottom than the Grand Canyon and who can run from sun up to sun set," Maverick replied.

"How much do I owe you?" Maverick asked. Mossy told him.

"Done," Maverick replied. He put the gold piece in the stable master's hand and then saddled the horse. He almost regretted leaving Golden. He liked it there and could see how he could make a future there in the last flatlands of the Colorado Rockies. He climbed into the saddle and rode away from Golden, as the eastern sky was beginning to turn pink with the rise of the morning sun . . .

~ ~ ~

Bud Riley stood in the street and wondered where Jonas Wilder was. He was supposed to be with Montero when they rode into town. Yet, at the moment, there was no sign of him. He was angry. Things hadn't gone well since back in Missouri when Oscar Bane had hired him and his gang to hit that wagon train. He didn't know why Bane had wanted it hit, only that he had. It was something that still troubled Bud Riley.

But the thing was, Oscar Bane was safe back in Missouri and Riley was hung out to dry out here. It was not a situation that the gunman liked, but nor was it something he could do anything about.

So, now he had to chase this Maverick fellow down because it was obvious that the man knew something. And whatever this man called, Maverick, knew, it was enough to bring Riley and his men down and reveal that they had been behind the local robberies.

~ ~ ~

Maverick rode north and west, heading into the mountains. He wanted to put as much distance as he could between himself and Golden. Maverick had a bad feeling, and he tended to trust his gut when it came to it. He had no desire to go up against those who had ambushed the wagon train, nor did he plan to cause them trouble, but it was something that came with the territory.

No, Maverick knew heading for the high lonesome was his best bet. Getting to the high ground ahead of his enemies was the best way to stay ahead of them. Mainly, he wanted to be left alone, maybe pan for gold or some such, build enough of a nest egg to buy some land and build a ranch running horses or cattle, maybe both. It had come to him that he knew a good deal about ranching and that he was a fighting man. The latter was the most important thing because it gave him an inkling of the kind of man he had been to make enemies out of killers and scum like that fellow back in Golden.

Maverick found an old game trail and followed it up into the foothills. The sun was climbing into the sky when he finally stopped to cook breakfast. A small fire to heat coffee and cook some bacon. He still had no clear memories, but fragments were starting to come back in little flashes as he rode. Back east, he had been a man of some influence and he had run afoul of some people who were murderers and troublemakers. They had burnt his house and killed his family while he had been away.

They had dogged his back trail and had finally caught up with him on the wagon train. They had thought that they had succeeded. Maverick was pretty sure he was willing to let them believe that he was dead. Then he had seen that fella in Golden. The man shoving the whore had just given him an excuse. One of the men that had attacked the wagon train.

If one was there, it meant that others were as well, and Maverick had decided to clear out, after knocking out the one that had followed him down the street. He was pretty sure that one had been one of the killers as well, but couldn't see his face well enough to tell. It was then he had figured it was time to get the hell out of town and put some distance between them.

~ ~ ~

Maverick eased out of the saddle, Winchester in hand. He had stopped in a stand of aspen trees about halfway up the mountain. He unscrewed the top off his canteen and took a long drink of water. He followed it with a piece of beef jerky, chewing on it to soften it some. Taking his binoculars from his pack he scanned the trail behind him. Two riders, not so far behind.

So, they hadn't given up yet. It said something about the quality of his enemies. Maverick smiled. He would have to make sure to leave no surprises along the trail for them. Just because they were persistent, didn't mean he should make it easy for them. Quite the opposite in fact. Maverick planned on making it as difficult and deadly as possible for them.

~ ~ ~

15

Back east, Oscar Bane sipped at his glass of sherry. He savored the taste, wondering if his men had managed to do what he had sent them out west to do. They had missed so many times, it was like the man had the devil's own luck when it came to trouble. He puffed on his thick black cigar, then tapped off ashes. The man's death would bring him a fortune, once he had proof. Money had changed hands with the promise of much more to come. Bane began to wonder if he was going to have to take up the trail himself.

~ ~ ~

Jonas Wilder and Bud Riley paused for a moment on the steep trail. They had found out Maverick had left town quick and had decided to follow him. Riley had a bad feeling about the man that had killed Montero. Even though, neither he nor Wilder had seen the man's face, he had a feeling that the man knew him.

He wondered if it was the same man that Bane had sent them to kill on the wagon train. Riley had thought for sure they had killed the man, but now he was beginning to wonder. What if that man had survived? What if he could identify all of them? If so, he could put them all in a hangman's noose, and that wasn't something Riley cared to contemplate.

About that time a bullet snapped through the air above him and took the hat right off of his head. Bud Riley bailed from the saddle, as another bullet punched a hole through Jonas Wilder who hadn't moved quickly enough.

Riley dug for cover behind a boulder beside the trail. Bullets chipped stone. Riley was becoming more and more sure that he should have never taken the job. A bullet took the heel off his boot and he drew his feet in closer. Nope, this job just wasn't worth the price.

~ ~ ~

Betty Grogan sighed again as she looked at the broken wagon wheel. She was on her way down to

Denver City. It had been her bad luck to hit the rock in the gathering darkness. She had known that she could risk hitting rocks in the darkness, but the thought of being caught alone on the trail at night had frightened her more. There were still renegade Indians that raided in these parts.

Now, she was stuck alone on the trail in the dark by herself. The very thing she had feared would happen had happened. Sometimes she wondered if people didn't create their own misfortunes by worrying about what could happen. The trail she was on didn't appeared to be well traveled but she was afraid to light a fire for fear of it guiding in either Indians or outlaws who might rape or kill her or worse, sell her into slavery.

While not totally helpless, the dark-haired beauty kept a .32 caliber revolver in the pocket of her skirt within easy reach. Her horses alerted her to the man riding up the trail in the near darkness, the moon and stars only beginning to show in the eastern sky.

He was a well-built sort, wide of shoulder and narrow of hip with piercing blue eyes beneath a shock of dark hair that barely showed beneath his black flat-crowned hat. His face was chiseled and handsome enough. He kept his rifle in hand as he rode closer. A cautious man, she decided.

"Any chance you would be willing to help a lady in need?" Betty asked.

"I might," the man nodded. "Depends I guess on why you need the help."

"I was on my way to Denver City to join a company of entertainers. Unfortunately, a rock in the road had other plans and decided to break my wheel," Betty smiled, showing her even white teeth.

"You're an actress then?" the man asked.

"Actress, singer, dancer. I've done a bit of it all," Betty smiled.

"And I am sure you do it well. All right, Miss, I'll help you with your wagon and even ride along over this part of the mountain to get yourself down to Denver City," the man told her.

"Do you have a name, Sir?" Betty asked politely.

"Maverick, Ma'am," he doffed his hat to her, as he stepped down out of the saddle to examine the wagon and the broken wheel. In another hour he had managed to lift the wagon on a lever and slip an unbroken spare wheel on it.

"I suggest you and I wait until daylight before continuing on the journey, Ma'am," Maverick told her.

"I'm more than happy you will you stay and guard my camp, Mister Maverick," Betty said, her brown eyes meeting his blue ones.

"I shall, Ma'am. Though after this I would suggest only public meetings," Maverick told her.

Chapter 3

Maverick sat in the darkness facing away from the fire he had built for them, sipping at his hot cup of black coffee. Mrs. Grogan was curled up in a bed-roll next to the fire. How had he gotten himself into this? He knew the answer. He had taken pity on a young woman he had found along the trail.

The stars twinkled in the sky above Maverick and he regarded them with some interest. Another memory came to him, his people had been a sea-going race and the study of the stars was something that had been almost second nature to them. He could name most of the constellations and their positions in the sky was something he had been schooled in since birth. He got up and moved out of the glow of the fire, taking care not to look back at it for that would destroy his night vision.

Instead, Maverick rolled out his own bedroll in the darkness beyond the fire yet close to the horses for he knew they would give him warning enough of anyone trying to slip up on the camp unexpected. He had fought Indians on the plains. He trusted the horse to warn him far more than anything else. He didn't have any trouble falling asleep.

The sky was turning gray in the east coming on when Maverick rolled out of his bedroll and added fuel to the fire. He put coffee on to brew, as he made biscuits and fried bacon in an iron skillet. It didn't take long before Mrs. Grogan was awake, as well. She moved a short distance from camp to perform her morning ablutions and when she returned Maverick poured her a cup of coffee.

"Sleep well?" Maverick asked.

"I did. Much better actually than I imagined I would," Betty Grogan replied.

"I'm glad I provided such comfort," Maverick smiled at her.

"As am I, Mister Maverick."

"Do you expect further troubles, Mrs. Grogan?" Maverick asked.

"I wish I knew, Mister Maverick," Betty Grogan supplied.

"I think that perhaps you should be prepared for anything," Maverick told her.

"You can never go wrong with that," Betty nodded.

"So I've been told," Maverick shrugged.

They cleaned up the dishes and then they got on the trail up in the mountains. More likely than not, there would be men on their trail. As far as Maverick was concerned, it was a given. He wasn't quite sure how Betty Grogan would feel about that if she knew, but he didn't intend to tell her.

Maverick knew that there were men following him. Men who were determined to kill him. He wondered about the woman he traveled with. Were they after her as well? It was a question that bore some thought.

~ ~ ~

Bud Riley frowned. He didn't like the fact that the man he was chasing had tried to bushwhack him. That just didn't set well with him at all. Nor did the fact that the stranger had managed to kill two of his men. He would find this Maverick, whoever the hell he was, and he would put lead in him. He owed that much to Montero and Wilder. Once he reached the rest of the gang and told them what had happened, they would be on the trail of this stranger called Maverick.

~ ~ ~

Betty Grogan wiped the sweat from her brow, as she drove the team behind the man she knew only as Maverick. He was a handsome man, reminding her somewhat of her late husband. He gave her a sense of comfort. Something she had not felt since Tom has been killed by the Indians on the way west.

Betty knew she could make a good living singing and dancing in the west. Especially, in the boom towns where the gold was being found. Tom had told her that much. Such places were hungry for entertainment. She knew that, and she planned for it. If she could hook up with a traveling show, her chances were even better.

When that happened, she would part ways with her protector. Because with the shows, there would be many others to fill that particular role. Especially for someone with her talents. Until then, Maverick, she decided, would prove a pleasant distraction.

He thought to himself that once they reached their destination, it would be easy enough to leave the woman in capable hands. He was sure the men following him had little interest in the actress. He still had no idea why they were after him. But it was something he intended to find out. First, however, he needed to get shed of Betty Grogan. He had a feeling that she would be more trouble than she was worth.

"Is there a problem, Mister Maverick?" Betty asked him when they had stopped for a short break.

"What do you mean?" Maverick looked at her.

"I get the impression that you don't like me," Betty shrugged.

"I haven't made my mind up about you one way or the other, Mrs. Grogan. But trouble is dogging my steps and I don't need to get you caught up in it," Maverick replied, shrugging his shoulders.

"I'd prefer not to get caught up in it either," Betty Grogan assured him.

"I suspect not, Ma'am," Maverick told her.

"You seem to have already formed an opinion of me, Mister Maverick."

"So what?"

"It doesn't seem too favorable a one," Betty replied.

"Why does that matter?" Maverick asked.

"To me? It doesn't. I could care less," Betty smiled at him.

"Why is that?" Maverick asked.

"Whatever do you mean?"

"From your questions and comments, you seem to be seeking my approval or disapproval for something, however, I have no idea what it might be."

"Perhaps, you are reading too much into it, Mister Maverick," Betty glared at him. Maverick smiled slightly.

"Perhaps, I am," Maverick touch his spurs to his horse and rode on ahead leaving her fuming behind him.

The air was crisp and clear and up on the mountainside, you could see damn near forever. Maverick watched an eagle soaring high above, riding the thermals on its way to who knows where. Maverick could admire the bird and understand it. Together they were solitary travelers.

Their fortunes would come and go, but Maverick knew that Lady Luck was the only love he would ever know. Despite the best efforts of Betty Grogan in the wagon behind him. For her, Maverick knew he would be no more than a diversion until she found someone who interested her more, or who could do more for her.

For Betty Grogan, he was a means to an end. Nothing more. The fact that he had recognized it so quickly surprised him. The trail led them higher. About noon, Maverick called for a break and they ate from some of the stores she had in the wagon. After eating Maverick pulled out the fixings and built himself a smoke. He struck a lucifer on his belt buckle and touched the end of it between his lips.

The burning tobacco tasted good. Maverick was looking to the mountains they were climbing into. Inside them, he knew he could find valley that would be good for raising both horses and cattle. Once he found the right piece of land, then he would buy it and hire hands. When he had that much, it would be simple enough to buy cattle or horses to stock the ranch. Then he could set to building a ranch headquarters that befitted the type of operation he wanted to build.

"What do you plan on doing after you reach your destination, Mister Maverick?" Betty asked, as he rode along the side of her wagon.

"Well, eventually, I plan to find some land and take up ranching," Maverick exhaled smoke.

"Cattle or horses?" Betty asked.

"Both," Maverick replied.

"Won't that be difficult?" Betty asked, sipping at the tin cup holding her coffee.

"Not at all. It all comes down to management," Maverick shrugged, exhaling smoke rings into the air.

"You have done this before?" Betty looked at him.

"I have. Not near as difficult as one might think," Maverick shrugged.

"I suppose not. What about those men that are hunting you?"

"They can come or go, alive or dead."

"Seems so simple, doesn't it?"

"It is simple."

"The west is a strange place," Betty shook her head.

"More than you can know."

"I see that," Betty smiled.

"I don't think you do, Mrs. Grogan. Not by a long shot," Maverick replied.

His blue eyes never stopped moving as he scanned the trees around them. The men that were following were still somewhere behind them. Maverick was glad of that.

"Why is that, Mister Maverick?" Betty asked.

"Because of the men out there are busy hunting me," Maverick told her.

"That sounds somewhat ominous," Betty Grogan told him.

"It does," Maverick nodded.

"Why is that?" She looked at him.

"Because life and death is the way of the world and the west, Miss Betty. There are no laws out here except the law of the gun. A man does what needs to be done and to hell with what happens back east."

"You really believe that?"

"I do."

"I think you might have a lot to learn," Betty rolled her eyes.

"Perhaps, you are the one with much to learn, Betty. I have learned what I need to," Maverick told her truthfully.

"Perhaps, Mister Maverick."

"No perhaps about it. Out here a man handles his own troubles. The law is few and far between. Somebody steals your horse or takes a shot, you best better be ready to shoot back, otherwise you'll be dead and eventually the law might get around to looking into it. You'd do well to remember that," Maverick told her.

"I suppose that is sound advice," Betty Grogan looked thoughtful.

"I'm going to ride back and check behind us. Wait here. If my trouble is on our back trail, I'd rather know it sooner than later. Knowledge is preparation," Maverick said, as he stepped in the saddle, leaving her to clean up.

Betty Grogan watched him ride back the way they had come. Maverick could be infuriating, but he had given her good advice so far. It might be wise of her to take it. Tom would have. Betty shook her head. She had been married ten years, before Tom was killed. She really hadn't learned all that much about men in that time.

~ ~ ~

A lone rider was coming along behind them, stopping ever so often to look at the ground and make sure he was on the right track. Maverick watched him through narrowed eyes and his binoculars. There were some boulders along the trail. He grinned. Life was about to get very unpleasant for that hombre down below.

~ ~ ~

Bud Riley took off his hat and rubbed his forehead on his sleeve. The sun beat down on him and made him hot, but the air blowing down off the mountain was cool. He shook his head. This territory called Colorado was a place of contradictions. He had just put his hat back on and put his spurs to his horse when he heard a loud rumbling from above.

Riley looked up to see several boulders rolling towards him, smashing down trees as they came. Riley gave a whoop and took his horse off the trail in a fast attempt to avoid the avalanche bearing down on him.

Chapter 4

Betty Grogan was back on the seat of the wagon when Maverick returned. "What was that noise?" she asked, curious.

"Avalanche," Maverick replied, as he rode on ahead of her. Betty shook her head. She would be glad to find some company that could actually hold a conversation.

~ ~ ~

Bud Riley snarled curses as he looked at the mountainside. The trail had been wiped out by the avalanche. He would have to find his own way up the mountain and then find the trail again. Shouldn't be hard since Maverick was traveling with a wagon. He had figured that much out. Riley built him a smoke. There were towns above him, some of them mining towns. He should be able to find out something. He set his horse to picking up the best trail up the mountain now that the main one had been wiped out.

~ ~ ~

Betty Grogan had added a heavier coat to her adornments, as the wagon had climbed higher. They entered a pass and the wind whipping through it was brutal and cold. Maverick seemed to pay it no mind, but she was shivering. He rode back to the wagon.

"If you have a couple of blankets you might want to wrap up in them. Night comes quick in the mountains and they will help you to stay warm until we get to town," Maverick told her.

"Thank you. I am getting cold," Betty told him.

"I thought you might be," Maverick replied.

~ ~ ~

The sun had vanished by the time they reached the town called Sundown. Maverick led Betty Grogan to the livery stable and unhooked the horses and rubbed them down and fed them. He unsaddled his own horse and took care of it, as well. He took her bag and carried it across the street to the local hotel.

Maverick paid for both of their rooms, though he made sure they were on separate floors. Hers on the floor above his. Anyone looking for him, he wanted them to find him and not her. Maverick left the hotel and headed down the street to the saloon for a drink. 'The Buffalo Hump' was a local watering hole and he stepped inside, moving to the right upon entering so that his eyes had time to adjust to the light. Maverick made his way across the crowded room to the bar.

"What will it be?" the bartender asked.

"Whisky and a beer," Maverick replied. He watched the bartender draw his beer and pour the shot of whiskey. Maverick downed the shot and chased it with the beer. He felt the alcohol hit his belly. Maverick leaned against the bar and looked around the room.

Nobody expressed any interest in him and that was a good thing. Anyone overly interested in him would mean that his enemies had gotten ahead of him. The fact that they had not was relaxing.

"Bartender, where is the best place to eat?" Maverick asked.

"The best is 'Josie's Place' if you ask me," the bartender replied. Maverick finished his beer and headed for the door. He stepped outside. Gas street lanterns were being lit and Maverick had no problem reading the signs by their light. He stepped out into the dusty street.

Nobody bothered him as he walked to the restaurant and ordered his supper. He figured Betty Grogan had taken her meal in the hotel dining room. The waitress was a hearty Irish lass with red hair and a sprinkling of freckles across her nose and cheeks. Maverick ordered some of the stew and a chunk of bread. He ate quickly and used the bread to sop up the remains of the stew.

Belly full, Maverick headed back to the hotel. He locked the door behind him and put a chair under the door knob just in case. His pistol went on the nightstand beside the bed as he stripped down to his long handles. Maverick slipped under the covers and closed his eyes and was asleep within moments.

~ ~ ~

He was up with the sun and quickly packed his kit. He planned on being out of town and gone before Betty Grogan was up and about. That woman gave him a right uneasy feeling. She might have lost a husband on her way west and that probably mean she was looking for one to replace him. Maverick didn't plan on letting any woman put her brand on him, at least not yet. Not until he knew for sure who he was and what kind of trouble was following.

The eastern sky was just starting to shine as Maverick made his way to the 'Josie's Place' for breakfast. The same Irish lass was working, and she remembered Maverick, giving him a bold wink after she took his order and brought him his first cup of coffee.

"So, heading out of town are ye?" she asked.

"Planning on it," Maverick nodded.

"And what of the lady that ye rode in with? Will you be abandoning her here?"

"We met on the trail. Beyond getting her to a town, I have no obligation to her," Maverick said. He took another sip of his coffee.

"Then she's not yer woman?" the waitress asked.

"Nope. Just another solitary traveler headed in the opposite direction. I've got trouble on my back trail and I don't want her involved," Maverick told her.

"Me name be Maggie O'Shayne, good sir," she told him with a sparkle in her eye.

"Maverick," he supplied the name he had taken. "A pleasure to meet you, Maggie. But don't be getting ideas about putting your brand on me. I'll be gone in an hour," Maverick told her.

"Well, perhaps if you pass back this way, you'll remember and ask after me. A girl could hope for no less," she said boldly.

"I'll remember you Maggie O'Shayne. You can bet on that," Maverick told her. She hurried off to the kitchen. Maverick smiled as he thought of her sassy way and knew that her invitation had been a real one.

He thought about it for a moment, and decided if he did come back this way, he would indeed look up Miss Maggie O'Shayne for his pleasure. She reappeared a moment later with his breakfast on a tray. She sat the platter down in front of him. It held a good thick ham-steak, scrambled eggs, three slices of bacon and two pieces of toast. Maverick was finishing his second cup of coffee, as he finished his meal. The morning sun was just starting to chase the shadows from the streets outside the window.

Before the sun topped the horizon, Maverick was riding out of town. The morning air was chilly as he headed up the trail. Maverick hoped to get across the mountain before the next sunset.

~ ~ ~

Bud Riley had stopped to camp for the night, and it had been a miserable camp. He had no food, no coffee and no blankets. It had been a very cold night. Bud Riley cursed the man that had done this to him. He was stiff as a board. When he found that damned stranger he planned on killing him slow.

He was tired and stiff and angry when he rode into town. Bud Riley tied his horse to the nearest rail and headed for 'The Buffalo Hump', only to find that the saloon still had not opened for the day.

"Where can a man get some food and a cup of coffee?" he asked a man hurrying past on his way to work.

"Well, 'Josie's Place' if you want anything edible. 'Scorpion Dave's' if you ain't particular about what exactly you're eating," came the reply. Bud thought about it for a minute and then headed for the first suggestion.

Several people looked up at him, as he entered the dining establishment. On one of them he noticed a silver star. Dammit! The local town marshal and that was trouble he didn't need. Riley went to a table in a corner and slid into the chair. A red-haired waitress appeared to take his order.

"You got hot coffee?" Bud asked.

"That we do," she replied.

"Bring me some and a menu," Bud said.

"Aye Sir," she replied, whirling away, not liking anything about the way that the man had looked at her.

Bud watched her walk away, appreciating the saucy sway of her hips, as she bounced away. She might make this stop over worthwhile if he didn't run afoul of the local law. He wanted a chance to ask around town first, see what he could find out about Maverick, the man that had caused him so much trouble.

~ ~ ~

Maggie O'Shayne shivered when she reached the kitchen. The man that had taken the table next to the wall was bad news. She could feel it in her bones. The way he had looked at her had made her skin crawl, as if he had grabbed her without touching her.

"Josie, can you have Rachel take care of the man in the corner? He gave me a bad case of the willies," Maggie told her.

31

"Did he say anything, grab you?" Josie asked with fire in her eye.

"No, it was more in the way he looked at me, like he was planning something," Maggie shook her head.

"I'll send Rachel to wait on him then. I'll not have one of my girls affronted by some drifter," Josie said, savagely. Josie sent Rachel out with coffee and a menu and then she stepped out to have a word with the marshal.

~ ~ ~

Nick Carson eyed the man in the corner. He had looked like trouble from the moment he had entered the eatery. Carson was a lean man with cold blue eyes and a thick mustache. He was also the town marshal and he had wide shoulders and narrow hips. Carson had built a reputation as a gunman long before he had started wearing a badge. Carson stood and approached the man.

"You headin' any place in particular?" Carson asked.

"Thinking on it," the man replied. He seemed none too happy that the marshal had picked him to have a conversation with.

"I think maybe you should finish your meal and get the hell out of town," Carson told him coldly.

"Is that right?" the man asked, leaning back.

"First one of your hands slides off the table and I'll drill you right in the brisket," Carson said, his Colt appearing in his hand as if by magic.

"My hands ain't going nowhere, Marshal."

"Good to know. Fact of the matter is, I think maybe you should settle up for your meal and get out of town now."

"Can't I even finish my coffee?"

"Nope. You ain't welcome here. Git gone now," Carson said.

"I gotta stand up to do that, Marshal."

"So you do," Nick Carson thumbed back the hammer. He watched the man's eyes. They widened slightly as the man realized he was bucking a stacked deck. Bud Riley stood and turned slowly, heading for the door.

Marshal Carson was a canny man, however and he kept a decent space between them as he walked Riley out the door and saw him climb on his horse.

"I see you in this town again, Bud Riley, I'll shoot you down like the dog you are."

"You have me at a disadvantage, Marshal," Riley glared at him.

"That I do, Bud. Ride the hell out of town now. I'm giving you a count of three before I start shooting," Carson said, his eyes hard and cold as polished black stones.

"I'm gone, Carson, but I won't forget this," Riley told him.

"See that you don't, Bud. Otherwise you'll be dead," Carson replied, the muzzle of his six-gun unwavering.

"Right," Bud Riley whispered, as he climbed into the saddle and spurred his horse into motion. He was still hungry and angry about that. Between Maverick and that marshal he hadn't eaten for a while. His belly wasn't liking that none.

Bud Riley rode out of the town and headed west across the mountain. The man calling himself Maverick was ahead of him. He knew that. The question was how far? He was no tracker. Bud knew that much. He knew that Maverick was ahead of him.

~ ~ ~

The sun was high in the sky as Maverick made his way through the mountain passes. He was glad to be starting down on another mountain of the Rockies. He thought about his time in Denver City. He picked up plenty of information during his time there, as Denver City had become a travel hub for the Rockies. The railroad had recently reached the city that was vying for capitol of the Colorado Territory.

Trouble was dogging his trail. He knew that for a fact. Maverick moved off the trail. He had heard that there was land to be had for the asking up around a mining town called Vail. He decided to find out if that was true. If not, he would find another place.

Chapter 5

Maverick paused in his riding. He knew that someone was on his back trail. He figured that the lady had no part of it. No, this was all on him. Maverick left the trail. He had a weird feeling, not sure what was causing it. A hundred yards up the mountain he came into a clearing. There were no animal sounds. Maverick halted his horse. The wind whispered through the pines, the sound somehow soothing. Maverick stood in his stirrups as his eyes surveyed the clearing.

Then he spotted it. The litters with the bodies. Most were pretty much gone, but a few bits of flesh still stuck to the skeletons. An Indian burial ground. Maverick closed his eyes as a hawk cried in the distance. He turned his horse and rode back into the trees. He had a feeling that crossing the clearing would bring more trouble than it was worth. No. This time he would circle around. Let anyone who came after him face the vengeance of the tribe. Maverick would not risk it.

He thought some about the woman, Miss Betty, that he had left behind in the small town. She would make out without him. Maverick was certain of that. She had seemed to be of the sort who could manage on her own.

Someone wanted him dead. He had to figure out both who and why. Maverick frowned. While part of his memory was gone, he still knew what he was. He was a man who was on a mission.

~ ~ ~

Betty Grogan was surprised to be informed that Mister Maverick had checked out earlier. She was not pleased at the news. She had been counting on him to get her over the Rockies and down the other side. Although, he had only committed to see that she made it to the nearest town. Now, it looked as if she would have to manage it on her own.

She knew that he was haunted by something in his past. She wanted to know what it was. Maverick had intrigued her. Tall, dark, handsome and very mysterious. He was a solitary man, just as much as she was a solitary woman. Both of them. Solitary travelers, drifting on the winds of change, flying ever free.

Like Maverick she was chasing shadows across the sand, emperors of no man's land. Lady Luck the only love their kind would ever know. Betty smiled into the rising sun. It really didn't matter. Lady Luck was the only love her kind would ever know. She headed for the café to get herself breakfast and some coffee.

~ ~ ~

Bandy Michaels kicked his burro in the ribs, bouncing his way down the trail. The old prospector has found a good strike and he aimed to file a claim on it. He needed a partner though to help fight the wolves off that might come sniffing after the gold. He needed a man handy with a short gun. Bandy weighed about a hundred and twenty pounds soaking wet, with a fuzzy white beard that reached down almost to his thin belly. He had on a thick sheepskin coat. His denim pants were worn and near threadbare in places, the flannel shirt he wore was in near as bad a shape, the sleeves rolled up to show the faded sleeves of the long handles he wore underneath. Faded red suspenders held his pants up and he had a Colt revolver belted around his waist. The holster was worn and while he could hit what he shot at, Bandy was no fast gun.

The sun was starting to climb over the mountains when he halted the burro who turned and gave him a dirty look. "Sit quiet now, Sid. I smells injuns on the move," Bandy said, his voice barely above a whisper. He pulled his battered Henry repeater rifle out of the saddle scabbard and urged the burro into the trees and off the trail.

Kiowa were not real big on personal hygiene, and their odor was one that anyone who spent time on the mountain got to know and know well. An old mountain man called Buck had taught him that when he first come to the Rockies.

Bandy stayed astride the burro just in case. Sid was a racing burro and could run like there was no tomorrow, if he needed to. And if a war party of angry Kiowa came up the trail, he would certainly need to. High above a lone eagle soared on the thermals. Bandy was quiet. He could hear the sound of shod hooves coming up the trail. More likely than not, a white man from the sound of it.

A big man rode up the trail, tall with wide shoulders and a wide brimmed flat-crowned Stetson hat. He rode a big roan bay horse that looked powerful and like it could run like the wind. The man had an honest but wary face. Bandy made a small noise with his mouth and the man halted his horse, eyes scanning the trees.

"They's a Kiowa war party out there. So far, we're ahead of them. Ride over here quiet and we'll see if'n we can keep it that way," Bandy called softly. The man nodded and silently urged the Bay over into the trees.

"You seem mighty sure of yourself, stranger," the man said. He looked Bandy over. "Prospector?"

"I done some of it," Bandy allowed.

"I'm Maverick," the man said, extending his hand.

"Bandy Michaels," he replied, shaking hands. He liked the cut of this Maverick fellow.

"That a Kiowa burial ground back down the mountain there?" Maverick asked.

"Shore enough is," Bandy replied.

"I thought as much. So, I went around it. I don't figure the man on my back trail did," Maverick said.

"Well, if'n he didn't, we won't have to worry about the Kiowa, but he sure will," Bandy grinned.

"Good," Maverick said, nodding.

"I guess now probably ain't the best time to be heading down the mountain then,' Bandy observed.

"Probably not," Maverick told him.

"I guess we better head back to my camp then. How do you feel about mining?"

"Thank you kindly for the invitation. Don't know anything about it, but I'm willing to learn," Maverick shrugged.

"You've got trouble behind you somewhere," Bandy looked at him.

"I do, bad part is, I ain't sure what it is or where it's from," Maverick told him.

~ ~ ~

Bud Riley rode into the clearing. He knew Maverick had come this way, but he had missed the fact that Maverick had backed out of the clearing and rode around it. He spurred his horse forward and was amid the litters before he noticed them. The blood drained from his face as he realized where he was.

"Shit!" Riley snarled. Hopefully, there were no injuns about. If there were, the odds were not good of him coming out alive. Just then an arrow slashed through the air, taking his hat off his head. Riley hauled back on the reins and turned his horse around, heading back down the mountain. If he had to take his chances, he would rather it be with the town marshal than with the Kiowa.

~ ~ ~

Betty Grogan looked up as a well-built man with broad shoulders and narrow hips dropped into the chair across from her. He wore a red shirt and a black

38

vest with a silver star pinned to the front of it. Dark brown eyes regarded her with interest, as he smiled at her from beneath a wide handlebar mustache.

"May I help you?" Betty looked at him.

"I certainly hope so, Miss Grogan. Do you know the man you rode into town with?" the man asked.

"Maverick was the name he gave me. What business is that of yours?" she looked at him.

"Marshal Nick Carson. I keep the peace here 'bouts. There was another man behind him. Bud Riley. You know him too?"

"I'm afraid I don't. I met Mister Maverick on the trail and he was kind enough to escort me into your town here. He mentioned trouble following him, but he said nothing more about it," Betty said.

"You're certain of that?" Carson asked.

"I am," Betty replied haughtily. She was beginning to revise her first impression of this town lawman.

"Bud Riley is a mad dog killer. I sent him on his way, but if he is after your friend, it's not a good thing," Carson said.

"Mister Maverick was a temporary traveling companion. Nothing more, I assure you," Betty said.

"Good to know. Will you be remaining in town long?" Carson asked.

"I don't know, Marshal. Are you asking me to be on my way? Alone and unaided through Indian territory over the mountain?"

"Not at all, Miss Grogan. Do you have a trade?" Carson asked.

"My late husband and I were traveling performers, Marshal. Do you have a playhouse in town?" she asked.

"We do. Are you any good?" Carson asked.

"You'll have to judge that for yourself," Betty told him.

~ ~ ~

"I ain't normally the type to pry, Mister Maverick, but the comments you made down below is somewhat bothersome. What kind of trouble are you running from?" Bandy asked, knowing it was the type of bold question that could get him killed if Maverick was a different sort of man than he had him figured for.

"Somebody wants me dead, Bandy. I don't know who or why," Maverick replied soberly.

"That's not an easy thing to live with," Bandy nodded.

"Nope it isn't," Maverick agreed.

"If'n you want to tell me your story, I figure I can manage to listen. You strike me as a man of breeding and good character. You're not the sort to be an outlaw."

"Thanks, Bandy. I'll tell you about it when we reach your camp. If I have to drag it out under the light, I'd just as soon do so over a cup of hot coffee and a plate of beans," Maverick said.

"Sounds like you are a man after my own heart," the old miner chuckled.

~ ~ ~

The band of Kiowa caught Bud Riley before he made it to town. An arrow in the back dropped him from the saddle and then they circled around him, kicking away his guns. The Kiowa weren't near as mean as the Apache or the Comanche, but they had their own ways of having fun.

They tied him up and threw him over the saddle of his horse and led them both back to the clearing where their people were laid to rest. Two braves cut some good logs and then sank them in the ground and bound them together to form a rough X shape. One brave tore the arrow from Riley's back, drawing a high-pitched scream of pain. The leader of the war party frowned. It was obvious to him that this man wouldn't die well.

Rawhide loops were soaked with water and tied tightly around Riley's wrists, and then were looped and knotted over the upward pointing ends of the X. They removed his boots and pants and tied his ankles as well. Another brave tied wet rawhide around Riley's privates and then looped it up around his neck, jerking it tight enough that it bit into his skin.

Yet, another brave brought out some honey from his pack and drizzled it over the outlaw's body and down to the ground, finding a hill of nearby red ants. The sun was high overhead now and it was hot. The rawhide contracted as it dried, squeezing tighter and tighter. Riley screamed as the rawhide cut into his skin, and soon blood was dripping down his arms and feet and from his groin and around his throat. The ants following the trail of the honey were swarming over his exposed flesh, biting and stinging.

Finally, the Kiowa grew tired of the noise and screams. The war chief drew back and hurled his spear into the outlaw's chest, killing him and granting him a merciful death that his broken mind had been praying for. As the war chief had predicted, the man had not died well. They left the body staked there as a warning to any others who might desecrate their burial ground.

~ ~ ~

It was getting on near dusk when Bandy and Maverick reached the old miner's camp and claim. Maverick unsaddled his horse and Bandy Michaels did the same for his mule named Sid. Both animals went into a small wood pole corral and eyed each other warily. Maverick gathered wood and built a fire in the rock fireplace while Bandy set about making some beans and coffee.

It took a bit to get it ready but soon they were sitting next to each other in front of the fire with a plate

41

of beans and biscuits and a tin cup of coffee in hand. "You ready to tell me your tale?" Bandy asked.

"Good a time as any, I suspect," Maverick replied, as he took a forkful of beans. Bandy pulled a bottle of whiskey out of a cabinet.

Chapter 6

"**M**y memory starts when I woke up in the remains of a slaughtered wagon train," Maverick said. "I was the lone survivor."

"How'd you manage that?" Bandy asked, looking interested as he scooped beans into his mouth.

"I got hit in the head with a rifle butt. My thought is that the men who were after me thought they had crushed my skull and killed me. My hair was matted with blood and it was all over my face when I woke up. Hell, I was surprised I wasn't dead."

He continued with his story, "It was a small train, only ten or twelve wagons. We had stopped for the night and knowing we were close to Denver, there were some celebrations amongst the travelers. I have flashes of the attack, I can see faces, but nothing after the attack. I don't know for sure but there might of been some renegades in on it, but they was led by white men. And I have the impression that the main job was to kill me," Maverick explained.

"Makes sense, 'specially if they wanted to make it look like an injun raid," Bandy nodded.

"Pretty much how I figured it. I woke up and everybody was dead. Most of them robbed as well. That's what told me that white men were behind it. I found some gold pieces well hidden in the wagon I was under, so I figured them for mine. I rounded up a six gun and a rifle and made my way to the nearest town which was Denver where I worked for a bit to buy my horse."

Maverick continued his story, "A man came in and I knew his face, knew he was one of the men that tried to kill me. He slapped a whore that had been friendly

43

to me, so I shot him. Another man followed me in the dark, and I stood him down, too. I shot another along the trail and sent a landslide down on the fourth, but I don't know if I got him. I figure it was him that was coming behind me and rode in to the Kiowa Burial ground," Maverick explained.

"If'n he did, he's dead now or a wishing he was. Them Kiowa, they may not have the reputation of the Apache or the Comanche, but they are just as terrible to their captives," Bandy replied, sipping his coffee.

"That's about what I figured," Maverick nodded.

"You figured right."

"So, Bandy, what can I do for you?" Maverick asked.

"I need a partner. Somebody who can keep claim jumpers off of me whilst I mine for gold. I've hit me a rich vein, and I aim to cash in on it. I'll give you half to keep claim jumpers off of me. And I'll teach you something about mining if'n you're interested," Bandy shrugged.

"I am. I wanted to mine so as to buy me a ranch and raise horses and cattle. Having gold will certainly help that," Maverick replied.

"I can see how's it would," Bandy nodded. "That's quite a story."

"Every word is truth," Maverick told him. Bandy looked into his eyes and knew that the man was speaking the truth.

"I believe you, Maverick. Seems to me, you need to find out who you were before you lost your memory and who wants you dead," Bandy observed.

"I know that, but I'm not sure I want to know. I have a new name, and nobody out here knows who I am," Maverick shrugged.

"Except you know. Can you deal with that?" Bandy asked.

"I guess I have to," Maverick replied.

"It ain't no easy thing," Bandy said.

"No, it isn't," Maverick echoed.

"So, what are you going to do?"

"I guess I'll help you work your mine," Maverick grinned.

"I appreciate that," Bandy told him.

~ ~ ~

Betty Grogan looked out at the crowd in the playhouse. She strutted out on stage and began her soliloquy. It was from Macbeth, not something that people were used to seeing from a woman. Yet, she delivered her lines with self-confidence and aplomb and the audience went wild. Marshal Carson was there to greet her at the end of the performance. He had to admit that she had talent, and one that would attract patrons from all through the mountains. Carson knew that she had already drawn players from several towns in the area, as well as local ones. He now believed that she was, indeed, a performer and not just a solitary traveler with no real connection to the mysterious stranger known as Maverick.

~ ~ ~

Nat Potter looked down on the camp. He had not been happy when Bandy Michaels had returned, especially with someone another man on horseback. No, he had planned on jumping the old man's claim while he was down the mountain in town. Now, that plan was out the bowl with the bath water.

Nat Potter was wearing threadbare homespun pants and shirt and a jacket just as thin. His boots were clodhoppers. His gun belt and pistol were the cleanest thing on him and were given far more attention than he gave the rest of his appearance.

His hat was battered down, the brim broken and floppy. A scruffy beard covered his face and his blue eyes were watery. He had a wad of tobacco in his jaw and he sent a stream of spit towards and open spot of grass. His sons, Poot and Clem were camped a couple of hundred yards back up the mountain. He'd have to let them know things had changed and they would probably have to take a more aggressive approach to getting Bandy's mine.

~ ~ ~

Oscar Bane frowned as he sipped his evening brandy at a saloon in New Orleans. Bane was on the move. He was going to kill his foe himself. He had heard nothing from Bud Riley or the others that he had sent after the wagon train. Kilburn had escaped him too many times. First in Carolina, then again in Ohio and Kentucky. His men almost had him in Missouri, but he had slipped away with the wagon train. Kilburn would not escape him again. He would hire more men and send them after him, but Gerald Kilburn was going to die. And once he did, his fortune would belong to Bane.

~ ~ ~

Maverick rolled out his bedroll in the small cabin that Bandy Michaels had built on the side of his claim. A creek provided fresh water and Bandy had dug a privy about forty feet away from the cabin. He found that he both liked and trusted the old miner and that was something that had not come easily since he had awakened in the burnt-out ruins of the wagon train.

Bandy had offered to teach him something of hard rock mining and he had decided to take the man up on it. Knowing how to extract gold from the mountainside was knowledge that could prove useful down the road. Bandy had also offered him a working share in the mine for helping protect from claim jumpers of whom there seemed to be many in the goldfields.

Bandy had been worried by some that he'd seen in a camp nearby. Maverick had heard stories of claim jumpers, lazy outlaws who preyed on the hard work of others and usually killed the ones that had found the gold and put their own sweat and blood into getting it out of the ground. He figured a bullet would settle their hash as quick as the next mans. And Maverick had no qualms about shooting any man that tried to shoot him first. A coyote or a wolf howled in the distance. Maverick closed his eyes and drifted off to sleep. The fire in the small fireplace burned down to embers...

~ ~ ~

They were both up before the sun and Maverick built up the fire while Bandy rustled water for coffee. An iron skillet filled sizzled with thick slices of bacon cooking on the stones in front of the fire place and the tempting smells filled the cabin. Bandy came back in with a bucket and filled the coffee pot. He added coffee grounds and put it next to the fire to heat up.

"You cook, too?" Bandy asked.

"Some, but I'm no great hand at it," Maverick replied.

"You've done some soldierin' in your time. I kin tell by the way you carry yourself," Bandy observed.

"Perhaps, I honestly don't remember," Maverick told him.

"Don't need to. It comes natural to some men," Bandy replied.

"So it seems," Maverick shrugged.

"After breakfast, I'll take you down in the mine and show you what's what," Bandy told him.

"Sounds good to me," Maverick replied. He was no stranger to hard work. He was sure of that given the rock-hard muscles in his arms and back, not to mention his wide shoulders and the slabs of muscle that covered his body. It was something that Bandy had noted as well.

"We got somebody watching us. I figure I must have messed up their plans coming back so soon," said the old miner.

"Claim jumpers you talked about before?" Maverick asked.

"Most likely."

"They probably didn't count on you bringing somebody back with you either."

"Nope. Most likely they figured to move in whilst I was gone. Now, they gotta figure out what to do next."

"No need to make it easy for them. You show me what to do down below and I'll do it. You can come back up and keep watch. Then I'll come up and spell you while you work down below. That way they won't have an easy time of it if one of us is always on guard," Maverick suggested.

"I like the way you think, Maverick," the old man grinned, as he poured them both a cup of coffee. Maverick took the crispy bacon out of the skillet and broke four eggs into it. He kept an eye on the frying eggs. When they were done, he dished them out and they both ate a hearty meal.

"You got an idea about who is watching us, Bandy?" Maverick asked.

"Most likely that no 'count Nat Potter and his boys. They've had their eye on my mine for a while, 'specially since I been bringing up good color. The assayer down in town seems to have loose lips," Bandy replied.

"Then after we deal with the Potter gang, I'll pay him a visit," Maverick said grimly.

"I think you might actually put the fear of God into him for sure."

"I plan on it," he told him, meaning every word.

The work down in the mine was hot and hard and took hours, with only candles to light the work. Maverick spent most of his time drilling with a hand-held steel drill single jack, a technique from experienced European miners. Each blow of the stout ten-pound sledge driving the drill deeper into the bedrock, a total of eighteen inches and busting it up to reveal the white vein of quartz behind it. The quartz was veined with gold. Maverick drilled out several holes and packed them the way Bandy had showed them to blow, then he lit the fuse and hauled his butt up the ladder, wanting to be on the surface when the charge blew.

The ground rumbled as dust flew up out of the hole in the mountain. Bandy had opened the windows and a nice breeze blowing through that carried the dust out the back windows. Bandy looked at him and grinned. "You're learning good," he said.

"Any sign of the Potter people?" Maverick asked.

"Nothing certain, but someone's sure been sneaking around in the woods over on the other side of the clearing, trying to figure out how they could get a good shot at me," the old prospector shrugged.

"Doesn't seem to bother you, them wanting to jump your claim," Maverick observed.

"It does, but don't do no good to fret about it like an old woman. Day'll come when my number's up. When it is, it is," Bandy spat tobacco out through the open window.

"One way of looking at it, I guess," he nodded.

"Only way I got," Bandy replied.

"You ever thought about taking the fight to them?"

"A time or two. But them Bald Knobber's seem to have a sixth sense about such things. They feel when trouble's riding their way and take off a'fore it gets there."

"Then maybe we need to make sure they don't feel it coming," Maverick said, off-hand.

49

"What have you got in mind?" Bandy asked. He outlined his plan and watched the grin spread across Bandy Michaels' face.

~ ~ ~

Nightfall. Dark came sudden in the mountains. A half-moon gleamed in the black sky above, surrounded by thousands upon thousands of glittering stars. A soft breeze blew, whispering through the needles of the lodge pole pines. The old miner put out the lights and Maverick slipped out through a back window. He was dressed in black clothing and wore an old pair of buckskin moccasins that Bandy had been keeping in his things. Lucky, they wore the same size. He carried his pistol and his Bowie knife, his face blackened by lamp coal and his hands covered by tight black leather gloves.

He moved like an Indian through the darkness, circling through the woods. Maverick knew that the best way to drive the claim jumpers off was to strike hard and brutally and put a deep-seated fear into their hearts and minds. He wasn't sure how he knew it, but it was something he recognized as a proven fact.

At some point in his life, it was obvious that he had been a warrior of very high caliber. He realized that he knew tactics and the best way to approach a battle. Tonight's action, while punitive in nature, was a battle that could win the war.

He crept through the darkness like a veritable ghost, leaving no sign of his passing. It didn't take long for him to find the first watcher. Poot Potter lived up to his name. Maverick smelled him long before he saw him. He caught the young man smoking, the bright red cherry at the end of his smoke was like a beacon in the darkness. Maverick was on him in an instant, the razor-sharp edge of the Bowie cold against the man's throat,

Maverick's gloved fingers knotted in his long unkempt hair.

"Make a sound and you're a dead man," Maverick hissed.

"I won't," Poot stammered.

"Good. Now, I could cut your throat and take your scalp, right here and now. Instead, I want you to take a message to your pa. I know he is a right reasonable man. Ya'll want to get yourselves gone from here and never come back. Next time, there won't be no warnings. I'll come in the night and slit your throats and scalp the lot of you and leave them hanging off branches around the Michaels' claim as a warning to anyone else who gets any bad ideas. You understand me, boy?"

"Yuh, yes Sir!" Poot whispered gingerly, well aware of the sharp steel that slipped a millimeter deep into the soft skin of his throat.

"Be sure you tell him, boy," Maverick repeated, and then he was gone. Poot Potter crapped his pants, but he didn't care. He hightailed it back to camp, completely unaware of the black shadow of death that followed him.

Nat Potter looked up when Poot stumbled into camp, a line of bright red blood across his neck and stinking to high heaven. "Boy, what the tarnation are you doing here? What the hell happened here?"

"A haunt near killed me, Pa. He said we better turn tail and run or he's aimin' to kill and scalp us all!" Poot wailed, not even trying to be quiet. Clem sat up in his bedroll, rubbing his eyes.

"What's going on, Pa?" he asked.

"Beat's the hell out of me," Nat shook his head. Poot was near in tears. He also smelled like an outhouse. Nat wrinkled his nose. "You shit yourself, Boy?"

"That damned haunt scared me, Pa. Said he would slit our throats and hang our scalps as a warning to others." Poot told him again.

"What haunt, Poot? There ain't no haunts out here!" Nat shook his head.

"Look at my neck and say that! His ghost knife done tried to kill me!" Poot yelled.

"Keep your voice down! You want them down in the cabin to know we're here?" Nat growled, his tone threatening. About that time, a stick of dynamite came flying in from the darkness, the fuse sputtering as it pin-wheeled through the air. It hit the center of the camp and exploded in a crash of fire and thunder.

Chapter 7

All three men were blown off their feet and the fire scattered to the four winds. A flurry of shots blasted out of the darkness and Clem Potter screamed, as a bullet burned his butt while he was diving for cover. Nat Potter jumped to his feet and grabbed for the gun on his hip, but a well-placed bullet shattered his wrist. He screamed in agony and Poot filled his pants again, as he scrambled for the tree line, unwilling to have his scalp lifted by some midnight shadow. To hell with Pa and Clem. If they wanted to die, so be it, but not ol' Poot!

Nat Potter was on his knees when Maverick appeared in the clearing like a shadow. He cocked the hammer on his Colt pistol and Nat Potter froze. Nat looked up and he knew he looked into the eyes of the Grim Reaper come to call for all the tortured souls that Nat Potter had sent to hell that didn't deserve it. Snarling a curse, he grabbed for his gun with his left hand and Maverick shot him through the head.

Clem Potter was on hands and knees, shaking his head as he looked up and saw a tall dark shadow scalping his pa. His stomach churned, and his dinner exploded out of his mouth. In the light of the few remaining fire's embers, he could see his Pa's bloody skull and the tall dark shadow was stalking toward him. Clem crapped his pants and scrambled to his feet running for the tall timber and not looking back.

Maverick watched him go and then he took the scalp and hung it on a tree branch marking the edge of the clearing. He was certain that once word got around they would have no further trouble from claim jumpers. Maverick headed back to the cabin.

Bandy Michaels had coffee on and waiting when he returned. He had rolled a smoke and was looking at him as he lit it. "Did it work?" he asked.

"It did," Maverick told him. He told the old miner what he had done and pretty soon they were both chuckling about it.

"You know them boys won't stop running this side of Bald Knob in the Ozark's," Bandy told him.

"That's what I was hoping for," Maverick replied.

The rest of the night was peaceful and they both slept well. By the end of the week, they had dug nearly ten thousand dollars-worth of gold to show for their efforts.

"How would you feel about hiring some good hard-working men to keep working this place and you running it?" Maverick asked, lighting a smoke he had just rolled.

"We'd need to make sure they was honest, otherwise we'd get the claim stole out from under us," he answered the question.

"I can pick good honest men. You're a smart man, Bandy. Can you teach them to be miners sorta like you did me?" Maverick asked.

"Taught you, didn't I?" Bandy growled, querulously.

"You did," Maverick grinned.

"I figger we can pay six men at least three dollars a day and the better we do, we can hire more and pay better. Most the mines hear 'bouts are only paying a dollar a day," the old miner blew out smoke from his corn cob pipe.

"I'll ride down to town tomorrow and deposit this in the bank. Make me a list of equipment and supplies that we'll need. We want this to be a first-rate operation, so we can attract first rate help. If I can find a good foreman, that will be a plus, as well," Maverick told him.

"Find a fella named from the Cousin Jack's, if you can, for the foreman. Those perky know hard rock mining better than most, and if you can get one worth his salt, he'd be worth any four others," Bandy replied.

A bit later Maverick mounted up, "I'll keep my eye out," he told him, as he kicked his horse into a trot.

"Never figured otherwise," Bandy rolled his eyes. "It's a small thing, but someone has to do it," the miner called after him.

~ ~ ~

Maverick rode down into Breckinridge, a Confederate sympathizing town named after the 14th Vice President of the United States. It was a pretty little mining town and held the territories first post office. He headed straight for the assayer's office. He had some words for the man. They weren't none of them kind. Maverick tethered his horse to the hitching rail and stepped up onto the boardwalk, heading down it to the assayer's office. The light was still burning inside, indicating that the office was still open. Maverick opened the door and stepped inside.

"You the one they call Maverick?" asked one of the men in the front office.

"I am," Maverick said.

"I 'spect you'll be looking for me," the man stood up and said.

"Why is that?" Maverick asked casually, never taking his eyes off the man's face. He had slipped the hammer thong off his colt when he had stepped down off his horse.

"On account of my boss wants you dead," the man said evenly.

"Your boss got a name?" Maverick asked, casually.

"None that you need to know," the man said, cruelly. Maverick hit him with a powerful blow to the jaw that shattered it on impact. The man fell to the ground, his face sideways, blood pouring out of his mouth. He looked at the two that had been backing the man.

"You buying into this?" Maverick asked, coolly.

"Nope, nobody paid us to care," one of the men answered.

"Probably a good thing," Maverick told them, casually. He pulled out the makings and rolled a smoke with his left hand. The quirley done, he tucked it between his lips and fired it, all with his left hand. The right hovered near the butt of his Colt, something both of the men noticed. They drifted out of the office and hurried down the road.

Hearing the commotion from the front office, a man approached, "Can I help you?" He asked. He was balding and a rotund man with watery blue eyes and a thin mustache over his upper lip. He wore an eye-shade over his eyes and he had to squint to see Maverick's face.

"You the assayer?" Maverick asked calmly.

"I am," the man nodded, vigorously.

"Name's Maverick. I'm Bandy Michaels' partner. I've heard tell you been talking about the high-grade ore coming out of our mine," Maverick's voice was barely above a whisper.

"Uh, it is a good vein," the assayer stuttered.

"Anymore lose talk will get you a bullet. I already scalped one bunch of claim jumpers. Anymore come around and after I finished with them, you'll be next," Maverick told him. The assayer swallowed hard.

"Yes, ah ... Sir!" the Assayer gulped, loudly.

"What's this batch worth?" Maverick tossed four bags on the counter. He already had a good idea from

Bandy but wanted the assayer to make it official. He had twice as many bags packed into his saddle bags, each of equal weight.

The assayer weighed the bags and told Maverick they were worth in excess of ten thousand dollars a bag. Maverick nodded and gathered the bags. He looked into the man's eyes. "One word, and your scalp will be decorating a branch around our mine," Maverick gave him a hard look and the man turned pale as a ghost. "Remember that!"

Assayer Joe Duncan nodded, swallowing hard. Maverick was a hard man, that was obvious, and he meant every word he said. Joe Faraday over at the town saloon paid him a lot to talk about the claims, but this was one time when it just wasn't worth it. No, Joe Duncan figured, he'd rather keep on breathing than say anything else about Bandy Michaels and Maverick's claim.

Maverick stuffed the bags of gold dust and chunks back in his saddle bags and threw them over his shoulder as he walked over to the bank. He had the assayer's written note about what each bag was worth. He deposited most of it in a brand new joint account that belonged to both him and his new partner, Bandy. When he left the bank, he headed for the local café for a bite to eat.

A waitress grinned from ear to ear as she watched him walk in. "A good evening to you, Sir" she told him. Maverick smiled in reply.

"It is a better one now for seeing your smile," Maverick told her, although he didn't know her name.

"You are one with flowery speech," she batted her long lashes at him.

"No one has ever accused me of being a poet," Maverick told her, with a slight smile.

"Perhaps they never bothered to listen to you then," the young woman smiled, as she arched one eyebrow.

"Why would they want to?" he asked.

"Because you, Sir, look like you are a fascinating man," said flirtingly, as she headed for the kitchen. Maverick watched as she swayed off to the kitchen. He picked up the cup of hot black coffee that she had poured for him and took a sip. It tasted damn good, a far sight better than what he and Bandy had been drinking up on the claim.

The front door opened and a man packing a star on the left side of his vest entered the café. Maverick figured him for the local lawman. He wasn't surprised when the man walked over and dropped into the chair across from him. "You must be Maverick," the star-packer said.

"I am. You asking or telling?" Maverick laid it out there.

"Asking. Word has reached us from that small town, Sundown, you left a widow woman behind when you rode out of town the other day."

"I did. I promised to get her to the town, nothing more. Word sure travels over these mountain tops," Maverick replied, flatly.

"That's what the widow told the town people there in Sundown."

"You got a name, Marshal?" Maverick asked.

"Marshal Allen is all," the man replied, extending his hand. Maverick shook it.

"I'm partnered up with Bandy Michaels on his mine. Rode down to make a deposit at the bank and hire some workers," Maverick said, watching the marshal's eyes.

"Lots of good men in town looking for work," the marshal nodded.

"They honest?" Maverick asked.

"Most of them," he said, nonchalantly.

"But not all?"

"Of course not."

"Can you point me to some of the honest ones?" Maverick looked at the lawman.

"I can. First man you should talk to is Evan Riley. He's over at 'The Wooden Indian' having a few drinks," Carson said.

"Riley a good man?" Maverick asked.

"He's a Cousin Jack. To hear them tell it, they're all good men," Carson shrugged.

"I'll talk to him," Maverick nodded.

"Keep your nose clean in my town and we'll have no trouble."

"Trouble is the last thing I want," Maverick met his steady gaze. He built himself a smoke as the man left and had just lit it when the pretty waitress came back from the kitchen.

"What will ye be having for dinner?" she asked.

"Give me a steak, well done with potatoes and all the trimmings," Maverick replied. He winked at her and she winked back.

"That will be my pleasure," she said coyly before retreating back to the kitchen.

Chapter 8

After finishing his meal Maverick paid for it, tipping the perky waitress generously and headed down the street to 'The Wooden Indian Saloon'. It was obvious from the moment that he stepped inside that this particular bar catered to the miners working claims on the eastern slope around town.

More than a few shot him dirty looks, but that had more to do with the fact that he was dressed like a rancher. The miner and some of the local ranchers had been at odds over the occasional stray head that had ended up in the camps. It was something that Maverick understood. Miners had to eat and if a cow wandered into their camp it was likely an act of God. However, a few unscrupulous men were rustling some cattle and driving them into the larger camps and selling them for a more than fair price. But the miners were hungry for beef after working underground all day.

Maverick headed for the bar and got a cold draft beer, taking a satisfying sip before turning to survey the room. There were many good men in the room. Maverick spotted the man he thought might be Evan Riley at a poker table, based on the marshal's description of him. There was an empty seat, so he walked over and sat down and joined the game.

"Where would a man find someone who knows about hard rock mining?" Maverick asked, as he gathered up the cards that had been dealt to him.

"Depends on why he wants him," said Evan Riley, as he gazed evenly at him.

"Most of these boys are panning for gold. Only the bigger companies are sinking shafts," another player added.

"Are they looking for hard rock miners?" a man named Sabre asked.

"Not so far," the man replied.

"So, who is the best and most honest among you?" Maverick asked, tossing two chips in to the pot.

"Some say this here, Evan Riley, some say Erin O'Doole," the other man replied.

"O'Doole is a fool. He spent a few days mining in Ireland before hopping a boat to come over here," Riley scoffed.

"What about Riley?" Maverick asked, gazing into the man's eyes.

"Riley is honest as they come, and he knows his way about a mine," the man replied.

"Then Riley is the man I want to be talking to," Maverick replied, taking two cards. They filled an inside straight.

"You got a legitimate offer?" Riley asked.

"I do," Maverick replied.

"Talk to me," Riley said.

"I will, but in a more private place," Maverick told him. The two men rose and walked to a back room within 'The Wooden Indian.'

Evan Riley closed the door behind them. He looked over at Maverick. "Well, Mister Maverick?" Riley asked.

"You know who Bandy Michaels is?" Maverick asked.

"I've met him. He's a man who knows his way around a mine," Riley allowed.

"That he does. He and I are partners. We have a good claim and we need men to work it. Especially, someone who knows hard rock mining," Maverick told him.

"That I do. Bandy's a good man."

"Will you take the job?"

"I will," Riley extended his hand. Maverick shook it.

"Can you find a crew of honest men to work the mine?" Maverick asked.

"I can, especially if the pay is good."

"Better than anyone else in the Rockies," Maverick told him.

"Then I can find your men. How do you want us to get there?"

"I'll take you myself. Once you're there and have looked things over, I'm moving on."

"Odd thing for a half-owner of a mine to do," Riley observed.

"He staked me, now I'm returning the favor," Maverick replied.

"Sounds like a fair deal to me."

"It is. Be ready to ride at sun rise," Maverick told him. He walked out the door and Evan Riley watched him go.

"There goes a hard man," he said aloud to himself. Riley stepped back into the saloon and started finding the men he wanted. Men that he knew he could trust.

~ ~ ~

Maverick headed back towards the only hotel. Darkness had fallen over the town. Oil lamps hanging from hooks lit up the dusty dirt street. Maverick kept to the middle of it as he headed for his accommodations. He expected trouble after his run in with the office men when he had first arrived in town.

Before leaving 'The Wooden Indian' he had slipped the hammer thong from his gun. It rode loose in his holster, ready to spring into his hand at a moment's notice. Danger was on his back trail and it was getting closer. Maverick realized it, but knew he could only meet it face to face. However, his enemies were not so scrupulous. They would shoot him in the back at the very first opportunity. He knew they were out there in the darkness waiting for him. So, he decided to make it easy. If they wanted to kill him, he was there, out there waiting for them to make the first move.

Maverick was half way to the hotel when the first shot fire out of the darkness. He dropped to one knee and sent hot lead towards the muzzle-flash. He hit the dirt and rolled as a second bullet tore past him. He thumbed back the hammer and fired again, a second scream echoed through the night. He spotted movement and fired a third time, and a rifle flew out of the alley to land in the dirt. He heard footsteps running away and climbed to his feet his Colt still in his hand.

Marshal Allen ran up, shotgun in his fists. Maverick looked at him. "They shot first," Maverick told him.

"So I heard," the marshal said.

"You want to see who they were?" Maverick eyed the lawman.

"Not especially, but I will," Allen groaned.

"Kinda what I figured," Maverick rolled his eyes.

"I told you to keep your nose clean in my town," Allen glared at him.

"I did," Maverick hissed. His hand hovered over the butt of his gun. He was more than ready to shoot the marshal whom he felt was as useful as tits on a boar.

"You draw trouble like crap draws flies, Maverick," as he shook his head.

"Not because I go looking for it, Marshal," Maverick said, softly.

"Doesn't matter, I want you out of my town."

"I'll leave in the morning. After breakfast," Maverick said, pointedly.

"See that you do," he spun on his heel and walked off. Maverick shook his head and headed for the boarding house. His troubled past was getting closer.

The men that had attacked him tonight were proof of that.

It was definitely time to be moving on. He would eventually have his show down, but he wanted to be on his terms and on the grounds of his choosing, not those of his unknown enemy.

~ ~ ~

The dawn of the morning found Maverick in the café having breakfast along with Evan Riley and six good Cousin Jack's as the Cornish miners were often called. They had worked together before and Riley guaranteed Maverick that Bandy would approve of them all. Maverick hoped that the man was right. The gold had been converted to cash and had been deposited in the Michaels-Maverick Mining Company account. Two of the men had loaded a wagon with supplies that Michaels had ordered, and Maverick had purchased, and Riley had added a few things to the list, assuring Maverick that they would make the job of getting gold out of the rock easier.

Maverick trusted Riley as a man who was good at his word, and if the man said there was a need, he believed it to be true. He knew he would be leaving Bandy Michaels in good hands with Evan Riley. He had enough legal tender greenbacks to buy land and cattle and horses to carry with him. He planned on finding a place on the eastern slopes of the mountains. Perhaps, back down in Golden on the river Cannonball Creek, renamed Clear Creek after the war of the states.

The blue-eyed waitress stopped beside him, her eyes slightly watery. "You're leaving today," she said. It wasn't a question.

"I am," Maverick told her.

"You'll be sorely missed, Maverick," she told him.

"Only by you, darlin'..." Maverick told her.

"I'll believe that when you send for me, but not until," she met his gaze.

"I just wouldn't count on that, don't put your hopes in no man." He told her.

"By the way, beautiful ... what's your name?" He asked

"I'm Julia, and perhaps, someday you'll think on this again," she said before walking away. Evan Riley looked at him.

"What was that all about?"

"Never try to read sign on a woman's heart," Maverick replied. He stood and walked over to pay for everyone's breakfast.

The men shuffled outside and got their mounts, be they horses, donkeys or the wagon. Maverick stepped outside, as well. The new day held promise, and he was glad for it. Marshal Allen stood on the boardwalk in front of the jail watching them. Maverick rolled a smoke and fired it up before climbing into the saddle. He threw the lawman a jaunty wave as he kicked his horse into motion. The wagon started rolling behind him as did the other mounts and out of town and up the mountain they went.

~ ~ ~

Bandy Michaels was sitting on his rocker in front of the cabin when they rode in, puffing on his corn cob pipe. Smoke swirled around the old man's head. "Evan," he said nodding to Riley.

"Good to see you, Mister Bandy. Maverick here tells me you've found a rich vein," Riley said, as he stepped off his horse.

"Light and sit for a spell, if you would. We'll be talking business soon enough. Coffee pot's on the stove and it's brewed fresh," the miner told him.

"Good enough," Evan Riley chuckled. He knew the men would appreciate the hot strong coffee just as he did. Maverick had told him the deal as he and Bandy had worked it out and knew his men would agree to it as well. Speaking to Bandy about it was just a formality.

One of the men hired was an excellent cook and had a job cooking even if he never cracked a rock in the mine below. Cooks were highly valued commodities in mining camps. He put together a lunch time meal that put the café in town to shame, and Maverick made it a point to tell him so. Finally, Bandy and Riley sealed the deal and after Evan Riley went down and looked the mine over, the others climbed down and went to work.

Bandy looked at Maverick. "You're leaving, aren't you?" he asked.

"I am in the morning," Maverick replied.

"Your troubles catching up with you?"

"They are, Bandy. I don't want them to cause you harm. So, I'm drifting on, but I'll keep in touch," he told him. He'd grown fond of the old prospector, but he needed to go. They spent the evening with the Evan and his men, laughing, talking, Maverick learning all he could.

Early, the next morning, Bandy told him, "If'n you ever need me, pardner, you call, and I'll come a running," Bandy looked deep into his eyes.

"I'll keep that in mind," Maverick told him, shaking hands. "I'm a solitary traveler, Bandy. Lady Luck is the only love my kind will ever know."

"Lady Luck is riding on your shoulder, my friend," Bandy said. Maverick tipped his hat and spurred his horse into motion, never looking back. No, Maverick was one who would always look forward to what the future might hold...

Chapter 9

He could smell snow in the air, as he descended from the upper elevations on the western slopes of the Rocky Mountains. He had no real name that he could remember, just one that he had adopted after waking up amid the burning remains of a wagon train that had been attacked out on the prairie. He had a vague sense that he had been the target, but the men that had sent to kill him had failed and he was only wounded and left without any memory of who he was. Now he called himself Maverick and he rode alone.

He had entered into a partnership with a miner and made some money, enough to buy a new outfit and equipment. He had a stack of greenbacks in his wallet that, once he settled up, would allow him to buy both land and cattle. Gold had been found in the Rockies and the rush was on. The men working in the mines would need food, and a ranch that could provide a steady flow of beef to the mines and to the soldiers manning the various forts that helped maintain peace and order in the western territories.

Maverick wasn't sure how he knew it, but he knew something about ranching and he knew men. He planned to find a good place for a ranch, and then find good men to work it. The west was opening up, and he planned on taking advantage of that. He pulled his heavy thick sheepskin coat closer around him as a cold wind blew down off the mountain. The sun was setting, and Denver City was still a ways off. He'd have to make camp for the night soon, so he began looking for a likely place.

Maverick found a cave and gathered wood for a fire. Snow was starting to fall outside as the flames sparked. His horse was happy enough to be out of the wind and he had a bait of grain in a feed bag to give the animal. The wind howled outside. Maverick pulled his Bible out of his saddle bags. Carefully, he opened it and started to read by the firelight...

~ ~ ~

Jonas Carr frowned at the snow falling. His men were tired and weary from the months they had spent evading The Union patrols after the 'War of the Rebellion' between the north and south. Sure, General Lee had surrendered, but that didn't mean that the Confederacy was defeated. Nope, they had come a far piece to keep the war alive. There was gold in a place called Colorado. Gold that could allow 'The South' to rise again. He aimed to gather enough of it to buy weapons needed for the fight, no matter what it took.

~ ~ ~

The Indian Chief White Feather ignored the cold wind that tried to find its way through his buffalo robes. He and his men were far from the rest of the tribe. They were determined to raid the white man's towns one last time before going to the winter camps on the plains below. He was a warrior just as had been his father before him. His son would be a warrior, too. Many of his people had fallen under the white man's guns. Soon many, white men would fall under his guns. The snow floated down, swirling on the wind. He could hear the spirits speaking to him, promising him victory in the coming days.

~ ~ ~

Gideon Shade shuffled the cards and spread them on the table. He had come to the boom town of Boulder located in the spectacular Clear Creek Valley. Clear Creek was a tributary of the South Platte River. With the snow falling and the wind howling outside the saloon, it was a slow night.

Most of the miners wouldn't be in before Friday when they got their pay for the week. Still, a few men came in through the week and he could usually scare up a game. Tonight was an exception to the rule. Jonathan Blocker, was the owner and bartender of 'Blocker's Saloon'. He brought him over a glass mug of beer.

"Quiet night," Shade observed.

"It is. Weather has folks spooked some, heard talk over at the country store today. Some of the old mountain men say a blizzard is coming," Blocker replied.

"Blizzard?" Shade asked. Usually, he spent his winters in New Orleans. This was his first time in the big mountains.

"Big winter storm coming. Colder than hell and snow up to your ass. Some folks say it took 'em a day or two to dig out of their houses."

"You ever been through one of them blizzards?" Shade asked.

"Once. That's why I got lots of extra cords of firewood laid in back in the store room and plenty of tin canned goods in the kitchen," Blocker replied.

"What do the miners do in these storms?"

"Don't bother them none, they work underground, unless they get snowed in. Most time they work in the warmer months," Blocker shrugged.

"Makes me glad I rented that room upstairs from you then. I don't think I'd like to go out in that storm," Shade took a drink of his beer.

"I reckon not. I'm gonna lock the door and shut it down for the night," Blocker said. Shade picked up the cards shuffled them again and began laying out a hand of solitaire.

~ ~ ~

It was morning. Maverick had kept a small fire going through the night. Snow had piled up over the entrance and had cut the wind, making it nice and toasty inside the cave. After he created a hole in the opening for ventilation, he took the coffee pot out and added snow and coffee to it before setting it on the fire. It took long enough for it to heat up, but it tasted good when he poured his first cup.

The wind was still blowing but the snow had stopped at least for now. He had a chance, maybe not a good one, but at least a chance of getting back to the town of Golden. When he passed through there, he saw that there was good land to be had in the area. Good graze for both horses and cattle. It was in this country that he had planned to set up a ranch.

Maverick sipped at the coffee. It was strong and bitter, and it woke him up, warming his body as it went down. He stretched and groaned, pulling a skillet out and frying up some bacon and eggs, he'd picked up on the trail from a farmer. He hoped to cover some ground today, making it at least as far as he could, probably coming in from the north at Boulder City. He knew it as a boom town, but he had talked to several miners on the advice of his partner and knew that the strike was a really big one but they speculated that it would soon play out.

Though he was only with them a short time, Maverick had spent a great deal of time listening and learning as the miners talked. Indeed, Bandy had introduced him to knowledgeable men. And he had soaked it all in. He took another sip of coffee as he pulled a flaming brand from the fire and examined the cave more closely. It went back farther than he thought, and he found an underground spring that formed a large pool and then disappeared down a crack in the rock.

The torchlight glittered off veins of quartz in the walls above the spring. Maverick regarded it, thoughtfully. He walked back to his saddle bags and removed a hammer and a chisel. He carried them back to the thick veins of quartz. He could see the glittering veins of the gold color within them.

He chipped away at the quartz, breaking big chunks of it off. He looked at it, examining it closely. Yes, there was gold in the quartz. A rich vein of it. Maverick broke up the quartz and extracted the gold from it. He chipped off some more. Morning stretched into afternoon and he continued to work. By the time night fell, he figured he took about three hundred dollars in chunks out of that vein. It was extra cash he would need to stock the ranch.

The wind howled outside the cave, and Maverick realized he would spend at least one more night there. He decided to work the vein a little more. Finally, glancing at his pocket watch sometime around midnight he stopped, having added almost another five hundred dollars to the gold he had found. Eight hundred dollars would buy a lot of cattle. Maverick smiled to himself, as he closed his eyes after building up the fire good. Drifted snow blocked the front of the cave, so the fire would keep it good and warm through and through.

~ ~ ~

Jonas Carr frowned. He looked down on the mine, despite the wind that was blowing snow around. His men were ready. He knew that they were waiting. He gave the signal and the raiders charged the mine. The miners had fought, but they had died quickly. Jonas Carr looked at the sacks of gold that his men had spread out before him. The gold would buy a lot of weapons for 'The South'.

"Boss?" Clyde Sooner asked.

"What?" Carr asked.

"Men are wondering what we're gonna do next," Sooner told him.

"We're gonna buy guns, Corporal," Carr told him.

Sooner nodded. "I figured as much, Sir. We need to rearm," Sooner agreed.

"Rearming is only part of it. We also need to build support for our South, Clyde," Carr announced.

"But, Colorado was Yankee country, Boss."

"Then we'll make sure they remember that 'The South' doesn't die that easily."

~ ~ ~

Maverick had cleared out the front entrance to the cave during the morning of the third day, the storm had moved on. The air was still crisp and cold as he led his horse out of the cave, the gold was packed away in his saddle bags. The wind through the trees was the only sound other than the breathing of his horse, as he began working his way down the mountain. It was damn cold, and he stopped in a stand of Douglas fir to build a small fire and heat up some coffee, melting snow for water. He only brewed a couple of cups and finished both of them, as the pine boughs kept the wind from him and the horse. With the fire, the small clearing had warmed up smartly.

Maverick felt like he could reach the town at Copper Mountain before he needed to stop again. The snow crunched beneath the hooves of his horse as he started out again. Glancing at the sky he could see an eagle soaring in the distance. It seemed like a sign. Another solitary traveler. Maverick smiled as he rode, letting the horse pick the trail.

~ ~ ~

White Feather and his men surrounded the log cabin. There were two or three outbuildings and smoke rose from two chimneys. The sun was just starting to clear the top of the mountain as he and his braves snuck up to the buildings. A door opened, and an arrow punctured the chest of the man in the doorway. He collapsed, keeping the door from being shut and the braves charged inside. Shrill screams rent to cold morning air. Several hours later, White Feather led his Indian braves away. All three buildings were being consumed by flames. Fresh scalps decorated their lances and coup sticks. This attack was just the first of many to follow. The white eyes would fear him and his name.

~ ~ ~

Gideon Shade closed his eyes. The wind howled outside the wooden structure. Logs burned in the fireplace that heated his rented room above Jonathan Blocker's saloon. The blaze large and hot, filling the room with heat. Trouble was coming. It came on the wind, and was something that he could feel.

Jonathan Blocker was glad to see the bar filling up again. The miners were a little rowdier after being cooped up in the mines for two days, but that wasn't a problem. Gideon Shade had a good game going and tensions had eased around town. Most of the boardwalks had been cleared and the streets were muddy with tracks from horses coming and going. Blocker was a big man and pretty much acted as his own bouncer. His arms were as big as most men's legs and he towered over everyone that entered. While he had a genial nature, those who started fights in his place usually awakened in the muddy street outside feeling like a mountain had been dropped on them.

Blocker had stepped outside while his barkeep covered for him. He found the chill air bracing and clean after the smoke-filled interior of the saloon. He didn't allow women in his place. Miners that wanted a poke would have to go on down the street to 'Miss Amelia's Palace'. She served liquor there too, but Cade, her bouncer, had a reputation for being quick with a knife. More than one miner carried scars from it from where they had gotten out of hand with the girls.

Personally, Blocker liked Miss Amelia and liked the girls that she kept. There were only one or two that could take him, and then not too often, so he wasn't a regular visitor. Something about Cade frightened him though. That man was just downright scary.

Blocker shook the thoughts away and took a deep breath of the cold air and let it out slowly. He was just turning to go back inside when he saw the rider approaching. The rider was dressed for the cold and he headed his horse for the saloon, reining up in front of Blocker.

"Howdy, can you point me to the livery and the hotel?" the man asked. He had an easy going way about him, though his back was ramrod straight.

"Livery's down on the next block, hotel's right across the street, 'Miss Emma's Café' serves the best grub in town," Blocker offered.

"I 'preciate it, Mister. After I take care of my horse and get some grub, I'll swing back for a drink," the stranger said.

"We'll be here," Blocker nodded, going back inside. The stranger kicked his horse into motion, heading for the livery stable.

Chapter 10

George Van Amsdol ran the livery and he was glad to see the stranger ride in. He was the first new face that the town had seen for a while. The fella wasn't too talkative though. He stripped off his saddle and rubbed his horse down good before leaving the stall. "What do I owe you for putting him up for the night?" the stranger asked.

"Two bits, and that includes all the corn he can eat," George told him. George was an old man with a pronounced limp. A thick black beard covered his chin, his eyes were a watery blue and his sun-burnt skin was wrinkled with age.

"Sounds fair. I reckon you can recommend a good place to eat?" the stranger asked as he tossed the old man two coins.

"Young Miss Emma has the best food. Miss Amelia's if you want the company of a pretty woman, as well," George replied.

"Food is plenty good enough for the likes of me," the stranger responded. The man took his saddle bags and his rifle and headed back along the street towards the eatery and the saloon. He moved up onto the boardwalk and stepped inside 'Miss Emma's Café'. Miss Emma was a winsome blond with long blond hair and blue eyes. High cheekbones gave her the look of aristocracy, though her long skirts and plaid shirt spoke otherwise.

Maverick decided that he liked her grit. She was young, not more than sixteen, but she was building a life for herself in this frontier town. She was the owner of what appeared to be a thriving enterprise. Maverick took a seat and waited as a young woman with long black hair came to take his order.

"What will you have?" she asked. She had waist-length black hair and wide green eyes.

"Steak and eggs, biscuits and gravy too, plus toast and jam," Maverick told her.

"Coffee?" she asked, smiling.

"Of course," Maverick smiled. The girl blushed before turning and headed for the kitchen. Maverick knew that she was near the same age as the young woman that owned the eating establishment. Both seemed awfully young to him. Yet, he was also aware of their interest in him, an older and mysterious stranger.

~ ~ ~

Ben Woodrow stepped out onto the boardwalk, buttoning up his sheepskin coat against the bitter north wind. As marshal, he needed to make his rounds the town. As early as it was, he really didn't expect trouble. Lots of the citizens had been busy cleaning snow out of walkways and boardwalks so they could get out.

Woodrow was in his forties, old for a lawman, but experienced enough to get the job done. His hair was sprinkled with gray and a thick mustache covered his upper lip. He had been the law in this town for more than a decade and done a fair job of keeping the piece. More and more ranchers were coming into the area, drawn by the good graze and water. Of course, the gold mines on up in the mountains didn't hurt either, for they would make a ready market for the ranchers to sell their beef.

His first stop was at the post office. The post master handed him a thick stack of envelopes tied together with a string. Likely the latest stack of wanted posters, and maybe a few newspapers from back east. Woodrow stuffed them into the side pocket of his sheepskin coat and stepped back outside. The wind was still sharp and cold as he moved past 'Blocker's Saloon' and headed towards 'Miss Emma's' to rustle up some breakfast. He didn't have anybody locked up, so he only needed worry about himself this morning.

~ ~ ~

Maverick had finished his breakfast and was lingering over a third cup of coffee when a big man in a sheepskin coat stepped through the door. Maverick had stayed alive being able to judge a man at a glance. He knew that this was a man to be reckoned with and pegged him as the local law. Maverick raised his cup to the man in greeting and the fella made his way over to his table.

"Morning," the man said.

"It is for sure. Sit and take a load off. The food's good and the coffees hot," Maverick replied.

"Miss Emma usually makes sure of that. I'm Marshal Ben Woodrow."

"I'm Maverick." They shook hands.

"What brings you to Boulder City, Mister Maverick?" Woodrow asked.

"I'm looking to start ranching. From everything I've heard and read, this area or down in Boulder seems like a likely place to build," Maverick replied.

"Lots of good land around for it, good graze and water. A ready market with the mines and with the Army setting up forts to keep the Utes in line.

"There's a fort nearby?" Maverick was surprised. This was news that he hadn't known.

"Fort Vasquez. A fur trapper built it originally over by Greeley."

"Might come in handy having the Army close. Have a lot of trouble with the Utes, do you?" Maverick asked.

"Not so much lately, but some of the young bucks are unhappy with reservation life. There's been word that maybe the Indian agents are taking advantage of their position and not treating the tribes the best."

"Have you passed that along to the Colonel in charge of the fort?"

"I have no evidence. Only rumor."

"But you are telling me. Why?"

"Because I have to live here," Woodrow admitted, suddenly looking like he had eaten something that disagreed with him.

"And I'm an outsider just coming into the territory and don't have as much to lose," Maverick met his gaze. Woodrow looked away.

"Something like that," the lawman sighed.

"Believe it or not, Marshal, I understand. I have no ties to your town. You've been here a long time. But I plan to be here in the territory for a long time. My question to you is ... are you so comfortable that you can afford to be exposed as a man who knew that something wrong was going on and did nothing to stop it?" Maverick asked.

Woodrow's face flushed a dark red and he got to his feet and stormed out of the café. The waitress came from the back with his plate looking confused that the marshal was no longer there.

"Put it down. I'll eat it and pay you for it. Seems the marshal lost his appetite," Maverick said. Her brow wrinkling, she put the plate in front of him and he attacked it with the same gusto that he had attacked his own breakfast. She shook her head and headed back to the kitchen.

It was nothing new to Maverick. He was a man with no past to speak of. His memories started with him waking up amid the destruction of a wagon train. He knew he was from the east and that people were trying to kill him but little more than that of his past.

He knew what he had learned from his partner in the gold mine about mining, but in that distant past he knew that he was a commander of men and had a good and thorough knowledge of battle tactics. Maverick also knew that he was not a man who trusted easily and that he had good reason for that.

He rode with his revolver loose in the holster and his rifle near at hand. Except now he was in a town, so he worked at curbing the instincts that came so natural to him. Maverick could read the weather. A storm was getting ready to blow in and he wanted to make sure he was in a good place to weather it.

~ ~ ~

Woodrow was angry. He was angry because Maverick, whoever the hell he was, was right. Woodrow liked the status quo. He had no real desire to go out and chase after raiders be they white or Indians. Woodrow much preferred to stay close to town. That way he didn't really have a whole lot to do. He had a bad feeling that Maverick was about to change all of that.

~ ~ ~

White Feather looked down on another town. It wasn't a large place, barely half a dozen buildings. But he also knew that there were mines located there as well. Those mines could hide a lot of fighting men that might be a problem for him. He didn't care. He would lead his braves to victory no matter what. The vision quest had told him so. White Feather believed in the visions. He would emerge victorious!

~ ~ ~

Saul Klein was the first to see the Indians riding down out of the storm. He kicked Lem Norton awake. "What the hell, Saul?" Lem asked.

"Injuns are coming. Let everybody know," Saul told him, as he stepped out into the storm.

Saul wanted to get a good look at the redskins, hoping to be able to tell if they were a hunting party or a war party. There had been plenty of both in recent months. He had him a bad feeling about this bunch. They looked like they might just be on the warpath after all. Saul knelt down behind the railing and lifted his rifle into a firing position. He hoped that Crenshaw and Morales had followed him outside. They had been his saddle pards for at least a decade. It would be a good thing if they were around for this.

"What have you got, Saul?" Mike Crenshaw asked, sidling up to him.

"We got hostiles out there in the snow," Saul told him.

"I figured that, Saul. What do you think we should do about it?"

"That's a goddamn good question," Saul admitted.

"I have an idea," Crenshaw said.

"How many people do you think will get killed?"

"I don't know," Crenshaw admitted.

"So, spill it. Them injuns is getting closer," Saul sighed.

"I see that. They look like they's a huntin' trouble, I reckon we should give it to them a'fore they open the dance."

~ ~ ~

White Feather halted his men, eyeing the mining camp speculatively. He and his men had been seen, he could sense the eyes of the men from the camp watching him, waiting to see what he was going to do. Some instinct told him that a frontal attack would only get his men killed. He turned on his horse and spoke to his people, then they headed down a trail that by-passed the camp. His expression was stoic as he made sure that the men in the camp thought that he and his band were leaving.

But leaving was not what White Feather had in mind at all. He had learned much of battle tactics from skirmishes with the white soldiers over the years. He and his men would travel far enough to hide their horses and then circle around and slip into the camp unnoticed. Once in the camp, they would take many bloody scalps.

An hour later, the Indians infiltrated the camp, darting like shadows between the buildings. Many times, they killed the defenders without them even being aware. White Feather had no illusions about them taking the mining camp totally unawares, but that is exactly what he and his men had managed to do. They had caught and killed all of the guards and then had proceeded to kill all of the townspeople as well. White Feather had swelled with pride as his men had attacked the camp.

Chapter 11

Jonas Carr was warm from the fire in the wood burning stove. He had decided to have his men rest in the mining camp until the worst of the blizzard had passed. The miners had plenty of supplies, something that he and his men had been running very low on before they took the camp. They had also secured every gun that the miners had carried before they had wiped them out, as well as their powder and ammunition. But even more importantly, they had found a good supply of dynamite and blasting caps. Those would prove very valuable indeed as they made their way down the mountain to raid other camps as well as the town of Boulder which was on the Platte.

Jonas planned on cutting a wide swath through Colorado on their way south to Old Mexico. Once there, he and his men would start buying arms and garnering support to rebuild the Confederate Army and strike into the very heart of the Union. He struck a match on his belt buckle and lit the cigar tucked into the corner of his mouth. The South would rise again.

~ ~ ~

The wind was howling outside, and Maverick took a seat at the table with Gideon Shade. The gambler looked up at him. "Care to play a few hands?"

"Not for greenbacks. It's too hard to come by this time of year," Maverick replied with an easy smile.

"You strike me as a man of breeding, Mister Maverick. I'd like to know your story," Shade said, giving him a smile of his own.

"Sure thing, Mister Shade, but you first. I insist," Maverick said. He hadn't gotten a good read on the gambler yet. Shade appeared to take no offense at his suggestion, killing time by dealing out a hand of solitaire on the table.

Gideon Shade considered the request. He really had nothing to hide, so he started to talk. "Not really that much to tell. I fought for the Union and once the war was over, I drifted west to forget the horrors I had seen during the war." Too many times, soldiers on both sides had committed horrible atrocities in the name of their leaders, himself included.

He had changed his name when he moved west, wanting to forget the man that he had been during the war. He had pushed cows some, even done a little mining but decided both pursuits required too much work. So, he had picked up a deck of cards and quickly learned that he was a natural at it. He got good at reading people just from the way they held their cards and the way they held their eyes.

So, he drifted, making a living at cards. He had worked the riverboats all along the Mississippi before moving west to the boom towns in the Rockies after gold was discovered. He was good enough that he didn't have to cheat. He was also very good with the six-shooter on his hip. There were times when folks didn't like losing and the fact that he was good with his gun settled most of those kinds of arguments before they got too far along.

He had drifted into Boulder before the first big storm and stayed, working the miners when they came into town to sell their gold and cut loose. It was a good place to live. It was friendly town and the miners that came in were good people. So, Shade had decided to stay at least until spring . . .

He finished with, "and that's my story," Shade shrugged.

"That's quite a tale," Maverick nodded. He had watched Shade's face as he talked and was pretty sure that it was the truth.

"Your turn, my friend," Shade said. Maverick considered how much he wanted to tell. Then he started to speak, taking a sip of beer before-hand.

"My first memories are of waking up in a wagon train that had been attacked by a group of white men either posing as Indians or there were Indians involved in the massacre," Maverick started. He noticed that got Shade's attention.

"I was the only survivor, but I couldn't remember anything, not even my own name. Eventually, I made my way to a Denver City. I had some gold coins on me and I bought in on a claim up in the mountains and helped work it. Once I had enough money, I decided to start ranching. Some of my memories have started to come back and I know that I was good with horses and cattle. So, I headed into the mountains and started looking for a good place to settle but I've settled on Golden or Boulder."

"This Blocker seems like an honest sort, do you agree?" Maverick asked.

"I do. Blocker don't take to too many folks, but he took to both of us. I figure that means you're a good man, for he isn't often wrong," Shade said, as he dealt three cards to the pile and was able to play all three.

"Blocker strikes me as a man of good character. The marshal tries, but he's getting old and worrisome in his old age."

"I get the same read of him."

"I'm not sure our troubles are over just yet. I've got a bad feeling right between my shoulder blades just out of reach of being able to scratch."

"I've had that feeling myself," Shade nodded.

"What do you think of Marshal Woodrow?" Maverick asked.

"He does a fair job of policing the town, but we've not had any real trouble other than them renegade Utes since I've been here. Mostly drunk and disorderlies, a few rowdy miners on pay day," Shade shrugged his shoulders.

"That's what I figured. He tried to talk me into bringing the Army in to deal with the renegades. He said it was because he had to live here. What do you suppose he meant by that?" Maverick asked.

"I've no idea, but it sure does sound curious. I reckon you want me to keep my eyes and ears open?" Shade smiled a thin smile, puffing on his cigar.

"I think it might be a good idea. I plan to settle here in the area and raise cattle and horses. It would sure be nice to know what my new neighbors might be up to."

"I like you Maverick, so I'll pitch in and help you out as best as I can. Probably won't be too much action around until this damn storm breaks."

"I don't figure so either, but you never know. I have a distant memory of being a soldier and being told to prepare for the worst and hope for the best. They seem like pretty wise words since they stuck with me through my troubles."

"I had a sergeant that used to tell me the same thing. He was right more often than he was wrong."

"A good sergeant usually is," Maverick said, standing.

"Where you headed?"

"I'm hungry and figured to head over to the café and get some food."

"Them gals that run the place sure are pretty ones. Do you think you might be troubled to bring me back a slice of apple pie?" Shade asked with a grin.

"I'll do my best to remember," Maverick grinned, as he pulled on his sheepskin jacket. He buttoned it up and turned the sheepskin collar and pushed his hat down tightly on his head before pushing the door open and stepping out onto the snow-covered boardwalk.

The wind had a bite to it that cut right through his clothes and the long handles that he wore underneath them. It was less than half a block to the café. But he was chilled to the bone when he got there. He stomped the snow off of his boots before stepping inside.

The café was warm and smelled like fresh baked bread loaves and pies. It was a welcoming smell. The bell over the door had rang when he entered, and the owner stepped out from the kitchen, smiling when she saw him.

"Have a seat and I'll bring you some hot coffee," she called before disappearing into the back. Maverick took a few steps over and took a seat, his back up against the wall where he could watch both the front door and the door to the kitchen. He was a man who worked hard at staying alive.

She appeared a few seconds later, a coffee pot in her hand as she approached his table. "Looks a little slow today," Maverick observed.

"It will pick up. Storm or not, folks have to eat, including the miners," she said confidently. She sounded like she knew what she was talking about.

"You've been through storms like this before?" Maverick asked, curious.

"We generally have two or three over the winter. You get used to them after a while," she shrugged, smiling warmly at him as she filled his cup with black coffee. "What would you like to eat?"

"Bacon and eggs and biscuits would taste might good. Oh, and do you have any apple pie?"

"Miss Emma baked a couple of them this morning," she replied.

"If you could box one up for me to take to the saloon, I'd appreciate it."

"I'd be happy to, Mister," the waitress flashed him a smile and disappeared into the kitchen. Maverick took a sip of his coffee, enjoying the warmth as it spread through his body. As he watched a few other folks appeared on the street, making their way through the storm. He watched as they arrived at the café and entered. Most were strangers, but a few faces were familiar. He had seen some of them the day before at the café.

Maverick had finished most of his coffee before the young lady got back to him for a refill and a tray bearing his breakfast. She put it in front of him and told him she would bring the pie back when she brought his bill. Then, she went to take care of her other customers.

He ate, enjoying the taste of food he hadn't had to cook himself. It was a welcome treat after days in the saddle. He took particular interest as a very well-dressed gentleman entered the café. The man was tall and slender and wore a suit cut from expensive cloth. He had about him the aura of money and power that was easily recognized. Maverick took an instant dislike to the man without so much as even knowing his name.

It had something to do with the way that he carried himself. There was a deep sense of arrogance and superiority that came off the man in waves. Maverick knew that he had met men like that back before he had lost his memory. Was that in Boston? He wondered to himself, surprised that notion came to him. But he didn't recognize the face, and he was sure that with the beard he had grown, anyone that he knew back in Boston would be unlikely to recognize him.

The waitress went over to take the man's order, flinching as he spoke to her. That didn't sit well with Maverick, but he decided to wait and see how she handled the situation. She took his order and was headed back to the kitchen when Maverick flagged her down asking for another cup of coffee. She gave him a weak smile and he saw tears in her eyes. He looked over at the man and frowned. His dislike was growing exponentially the longer he watched the man. Other townsfolk either avoided him altogether, or genuflected as if he was someone of unbridled importance.

About that time, Marshal Woodrow entered, and Maverick waved him over to his table. He noticed that the man ignored the marshal as if he was beneath his notice. Maverick was curious about that.

"Mister Maverick, to what do I owe the pleasure?" Woodrow asked, as he reached him.

"Have a seat, Marshal. I've got a few more questions about Boulder and Golden and the rangeland around here," Maverick told him. The waitress returned to refill his cup, her composure restored.

"Marshal Woodrow, would you like some coffee, as well?" she asked.

"Sure thing, Macy. I'd appreciate it," Woodrow told her with a smile. Macy filled a cup and sat it in front of him and returned his smile before moving away to care for her other customers. Maverick noticed that she kept her distance from the man that had put tears in her eyes.

"So, what would you like to know, Mister Maverick?" Woodrow asked.

"How many ranches are there around the area?" Maverick asked, keeping an eye on the girl named Macy.

"Half a dozen small ones and one big ranch. Silas Marcum owns it. Barrel M. Biggest ranch in the territory," Woodrow replied, before taking a sip of the hot coffee.

"What do the other ranchers think of him?" Maverick asked. He watched Macy return to the kitchen.

"If you want the honest answer, they don't much care for him. Marcum came in and bought up a bunch of prime graze lands with water and set up shop. Nobody knows where his money comes from, but it's assumed that he got it after the war. Marcum isn't the most talkative sort about things like that either," Woodrow explained.

"Sounds like somebody needs to take him down a peg or two," Maverick noted.

"A couple of the smaller ranchers tried. Both of them are buried up on Boot Hill, our local cemetery. All strictly legal. It seems Marcum is handy with a pistol and the men that challenged him weren't. He killed them in fair fights right out on Main Street and there wasn't a damn thing I could do about it. Not within the law, anyway."

"How do you think he'll feel about me coming in and buying up a big chunk of range?"

"Off hand, I suspect he won't be too happy about it."

"Good. I don't want him to be happy about it," Maverick replied with a wicked grin.

Chapter 12

"Why is that, Maverick? If you don't mind me asking that is," Woodrow looked at him.

"Is that Marcum over there?" Maverick motioned to the obnoxious well-dressed man that had made Macy cry. Woodrow craned his neck to look and see who Maverick was pointing at. He turned his head back around quickly.

"It is," Woodrow confirmed.

"I don't like him," Maverick shrugged. "Don't worry, I ain't here to start trouble, but I get riled up by people who run rough-shod over others."

"He does have a reputation for that."

"I've seen how he treats the young women that run this eatery. I plan to call him on it," Maverick said. He watched closely as Macy carried the man's food to his table and put it down in front of him. The man made a low-voiced comment that sent Macy spinning around and rushing back to the kitchen.

"That's enough," Maverick said, standing up suddenly and pushing past the marshal and headed straight for Silas Marcum. Maverick crossed the distance in three long steps and reached around, grabbing Marcum by his collar and yanking him to his feet before smashing a hard-knuckled fist into the man's mouth, busting his lip and sending him stumbling towards the door. Maverick quickly closed the distance and hit him again, this time in the gut and doubling him over. A man that had been about to step inside saw what was coming and stepped back out just as Maverick swung from the floor and smashed Marcum's jaw, sending him out through the open door.

Marcum lay in the snow and groaned for a moment as blowing snow chilled his skin then he opened his eyes and looked at the big man standing over him. "If I ever see you mistreat either of those girls inside again, I'll kill you," Maverick said.

"Who the hell are you?" Silas asked, as his wits started to return. Laying on his back, he edged his hand towards his gun.

"The name is Maverick. You want to try me, go for it. It'll give me the excuse I need to go ahead and kill you."

"I don't buck a stacked deck, Mister," Marcum rubbed his mouth, looking at the blood on his hand. "I'll not forget this, Maverick."

"I hope not," Maverick said, before turning around and walking back into the restaurant. Marcum struggled to his feet and lurched down the street to the livery where he had left his horse. Maverick, eh? Well, Maverick had just made the biggest mistake of his life.

~ ~ ~

Oscar Bane Had arrived in the Colorado Territory. He lowered his glass of sherry and frowned at the man sitting across from him. "What do you mean you have never heard of Gerald Kilburn?" he demanded.

"Ain't nobody by that name even come through here in Denver City, Mister Bane," Luke Hammond replied.

"You're absolutely certain of that?"

"I am, Mister Bane. There was a man that fit the description, but he was calling himself Maverick. Could that be him?"

"What did he look like?"

"Tall, muscular, dark hair. He's looking to buy land and go into ranching."

"That could be him. Do you know where he was heading?"

"He said something about looking for some land over in Golden or Boulder before he went into the mountains."

"That still takes in a lot of territory."

"It's all I've got, Mister Bane. But with this blizzard that has settled in, there ain't much else to be done."

"Luke, I want you to round me up a team of man-hunters. Ones that are not too particular about their prey," Bane told him.

"I'll find the men you need, Mister Bane," Hammond told him.

"I hope so," Bane said.

~ ~ ~

Jonas Carr looked out at the storm. The winds were starting to die down. The snow wasn't falling as hard either. The blizzard was coming to an end. That meant that they would soon be moving on. According to the map there was a town nearby called Breckinridge. It even had a bank. Carr smiled. That bank was about to help the cause of 'The South'.

Clyde Sooner took a seat across from Carr. "How much do you know about this town, Clyde?" Carr asked.

"Only what Jimmy told me. A nice size town, some stores, a few of saloons, cafés, livery stable, and banks. They gotta old man for a town marshal to keep the peace, but not a whole lot goes on there. There are some ranches in the area as well as half a dozen gold mines. For the moment, it is the only place that the miners have to ship their gold from," Sooner replied.

"And Jimmy is sure about this?" Carr asked.

"He is, you see, 'cause Jimmy worked for one of the big spreads a'fore the war. Jimmy Breslin was a top hand working for a fella named Silas Marcum over in Boulder."

"Does Jimmy know if this Marcum fella might be sympathetic with our cause?" Carr asked, thoughtfully.

"You'd have to ask Jimmy about that. I don't reckon he ever mentioned one way or another," Sooner shrugged.

"Find out. It might be good to have an ally in place when we hit the town," Carr instructed. Sooner nodded and rose before walking out. Carr fired up a new cigar after biting the end off of it and spitting it onto the floor. If this Silas Marcum would agree to work with them, the return of 'The South' might come even quicker.

~ ~ ~

"Oh, Mister Maverick, why did you do that?" Macy asked, her face a mask of fear.

"I did it because you don't deserve to be treated like that and, Silas Marcum is a bully. I don't like bullies." Maverick told her calmly.

"He might try and burn this place down," Macy shook her head.

"If he does, he'll have to go through me. He'll be dead if he tries that," Maverick said, in a matter-of-fact tone that brooked no argument.

"If he makes a move against you or Emma either one, Macy, I'll lock him up. If I fail in that, Maverick will take care of things. This town needs you girls a hell of a lot more than we need Silas Marcum," Woodrow told her.

"I don't know what to say," Macy wiped tears from her eyes.

"Then how about getting us some more coffee?" Maverick grinned at her.

"I can do that. This one is on the house," Macy told him, thankfully.

"Do you have a land office in town?" Maverick asked.

"Of course, Joe Stacy runs it. You want me to show you, after you finish your meal?" Woodrow asked.

"I'd like that," Maverick told him.

~ ~ ~

Silas Marcum was fit to be tied, as he rode out of town and back towards his ranch. The snow had stopped falling and was now just blowing on the driving wind. The wind had a bite to it, but he was too angry to pay attention to it. It had been a long time since anybody had talked to him like that. Or had manhandled him in such a way. The man calling himself Maverick was going to pay for that. As were the two girls that ran the café. By the time Marcum had reached the gate leading to the Barrel M, his face was too numb to hurt, and his anger had cooled some. Not so much that he would forget the disservice that had been done to him. But he was now cool-headed enough to plan his revenge and how he would kill the man calling himself Maverick.

~ ~ ~

"Well, let me consult the county map, Mister Maverick," Joe Stacy told him.

"I want to start with a couple of hundred acres of land with good graze and water, Mister Stacy. I aim to run both cattle and horses on my range," Maverick replied. Stacy had struck him as being honest enough, but there was something about the man that didn't sit quite right.

"There is plenty of good land along the three Boulder Creeks that should meet your criteria," Stacy said

"It should. Does it flood much?"

"Sometimes a little during the spring run-off," Stacy admitted.

"How bad?"

"Less than you might expect."

"Draw me up a deed, Mister Stacy. But you put a provision in the bill of sale. If it isn't exactly as represented, you'll buy it back for the same price you sold it to me for."

"I'm sorry what? I've never heard of such a thing!" Stacy puffed up.

"I don't like being set up to be swindled either, Mister Stacy," Maverick told him, his voice suddenly cold and hard.

"Swindled? Are you calling me a crook?"

"I am, Sir. I want prime land, land that borders the Barrel M. You see, I checked on you before I left to ride over here. I guess you didn't expect that," Maverick told him.

"I have no idea what you are talking about," Stacy blustered.

"Vic Stemple and Maury King tell a different story. You had already sold them that stretch of land knowing it floods so bad that it's useless for ranching. Vic and I rode together for a short time during the war and he warned me about you. I just had to see it for myself. Now, show me some good land, or I'll let the marshal know all about you," Maverick smiled.

"Fine," Stacy harrumphed. Half an hour later, Maverick left the land office with a deed in hand for the land he had already looked at and chosen earlier. It was five-hundred acres that bordered the Barrel M and had plenty of good graze and water. He would bring cattle in during the spring and summer and a lot of horses, too. He registered his brand as well, it was a long-horned cow head. The Maverick brand.

Maverick carried the pie back to Jonathan Blocker's place and sat it down on the table in front of Gideon Shade.

"Took you long enough," Shade growled.

"I had business to attend to," Maverick replied.

"What kind of business?"

"I bought land for a ranch."

"In the middle of winter?"

"Yep. I also busted Silas Marcum in the mouth and threw him out of the café after he made Miss Macy cry."

"By my sainted Mother, I'd have paid to see that!" Jonathan Blocker chuckled, sounding a lot like a bear roaring in a deep cave.

"For that matter, so would I," Gideon Shade chuckled. "Jonathan, pour Maverick a drink. I think he deserves it after that."

"Agreed," Blocker nodded.

Pretty soon, some of the townspeople drifted in and they told the same story that Maverick had about tossing Marcum out into the snow. Gideon Shade and Jonathan Blocker shook their heads in awe. Maverick had retired upstairs to his room.

The wind continued to howl past the buildings outside, but it had stopped snowing. Now, the snow was just blowing around and drifting up against buildings. The drifted snow provided insulation for the buildings against the wind and folks settled in. Soon, the storm would pass and life in Boulder would go back to normal. At least that was what they had thought.

~ ~ ~

In Denver City, Oscar Bane sat quietly in his room at the Golden Nugget Hotel drinking brandy and contemplating his plans for the future. He had hired a crew to trace Maverick's trail and to kill him. It would take some time, especially with the storm that had just blown through the area. But they were all seasoned manhunters and he had no doubt that they would find the man that was now calling himself Maverick. He had put up a hundred thousand-dollar bounty on Maverick. Whoever brought him his head would get the prize. Bane fired up another cigar and sipped at the brandy once more. It had an apple taste to it and was quite enjoyable to the pallet. Once Maverick was dead, his fortune would belong to Oscar Bane.

Chapter 13

"The storm has finally passed, Boss," Clyde Sooner announced, as he entered the warm cave cut back into the mountain behind the wooden house that masked it.

"How bad are the trails?" Jonas Carr asked, sipping from a bottle of whiskey.

"Covered with snow and ice, but if we give them a couple of days and take it slow we can probably make it down to Boulder."

"Send Jimmy on ahead to talk to that Silas Marcum fellow and see if he is amicable to our cause. I want to know by the time we reach Boulder," Carr ordered.

"I'll send him," Sooner replied turning and leaving Major Jonas Carr alone with his thoughts. Clyde was worried about him. He hadn't been the same since the war had ended and the Confederacy had surrendered. It was like something had broken inside his head. He didn't always agree with what he did, but Major Carr had saved his life more than once on the battlefield. So, he owed it to him to stay with the major and protect him as best he could.

~ ~ ~

Maverick was up early the next morning and made his way to the café for breakfast. The food was worth it, as were the two young ladies that ran the place. But he had a lot to accomplish today. The first of which was riding out again to see the land that he had purchased, bordered on one side by the river. There were more people in the café this morning. It was good to see the place this busy. He had been a little worried about his impetuous behavior the day before. Apparently, word had spread given the smiles and greetings that he was receiving when he walked in. It looked like most of the town folk had accepted him, which spoke volumes about how much they disliked Silas Marcum.

"Good Morning, Mister Maverick!" Macy called from across the room, giving him a dazzling smile as she rushed to seat him at a table near the back where he would be against the wall. He hadn't realized just how canny the girl was up to that point. She poured him a cup of coffee and waited for his order. He gave it to her and she quickly disappeared into the kitchen.

Not too long after, a cowboy sauntered in, his eyes sweeping the room and lighting on Maverick. Maverick recognized the scrutiny and let it slip off him like water off a duck's back. He sipped his coffee, as the younger man made his way across the room and took a seat across from him. "Howdy," the young cowboy said. From appearances, he wasn't more than seventeen or eighteen years old.

"Howdy. Do I know you, Son?" Maverick asked, taking a sip of his coffee.

"No reason you should, Sir. I heard you bought some land and I'm looking for work. Thought maybe you might have a job for me," the kid shrugged.

"It's possible. The work will be hard and the hours long, but I'll pay you a fair wage for a solid day of work. You got a name?" Maverick asked.

"Luke Cantrell, Mister Maverick. I'm courting Miss Emma and I figure I got a better chance with a steady job," the boy told him.

"I'd say that's some smart thinking, Luke. I'm planning on riding out again to look over the land I bought after breakfast. You're welcome to ride along with me," Maverick responded.

"I'm obliged, Mister Maverick. Work hereabouts is hard to come by in the winter unless you're willing to dig under the ground like a mole. I dislike being in closed up spaces, so that ain't no life for me," Luke shook his head.

"I understand that and don't fault you for it. Working in mines takes a special breed, and while I've done it, I have no real love for it. Give me wide open pastures and mountain meadows anytime," Maverick told him.

Just then Macy arrived with two plates. She put one in front of Maverick and one in front of Luke. "Emma saw you come in, she knows what you like," she told the young cowboy with a smile before returning to the back and reappearing with a coffee pot that she went around the room refilling cups from.

"I'd say Emma cares about you," Maverick observed with a grin, watching Luke's face turn a bit red.

"I reckon you'd be right about that. I care a lot about her as well."

"Then eat up, Lad. We've got work ahead of us this day," Maverick told him.

~ ~ ~

Roger Colton rode into Denver City following the storm. Folks were starting to dig out and paths had been cleared down the middle of the busiest streets. Colton had gotten word that Oscar Bane wanted to hire him. He had worked for Bane before and it had been profitable for him. Colton liked good paying work.

He had been surprised to find out that Bane was in Denver City rather than St. Louis, and he wondered what had drawn the man so far west. But then Denver was a growing town and there was money to be made here, especially since gold had been discovered all over up in the Rockies. There were already a railroad lines coming into Denver and the lines were crossing further west into the Nevada and California territories, as well.

Colton headed for the livery stable and took care of his horse first. Then carrying his rifle and saddlebags, he hurried back along the main street to the Golden Nugget Hotel. That was where Bane was supposed to be staying and where a room was supposed to be reserved for Colton.

It was a whole lot warmer inside the hotel than it was on the street. He had stomped the snow off of his boots before coming inside. Once inside, he shook the snow off his Stetson and shrugged it off the shoulders of his Mackinaw jacket before heading across the waxed hardwood floors to the reception desk.

There was a man sitting behind it in a white shirt with sleeve garters and a visor over his round glasses. He had a thin mustache covering his top lip and his brown hair was thinning enough to see scalp gleaming through the top.

"You have a room reserved for me, name is Roger Colton," he asked the desk clerk.

"Ah, yes, Mister Colton. I have you right here. Room two eight. On the second floor and in the back," the desk clerk told him, handing him the key.

"Thanks," Colton said as he took the key and headed for the stairs. He aimed to rest up a mite before tracking down Bane. He wanted to be refreshed and clear headed when they met.

~ ~ ~

Maverick and Luke Cantrell had ridden out to the land he had bought. He had asked Luke a lot of questions about the land and the area and the boy had proven to have a wealth of knowledge about the area and the land that Maverick had purchased. Luke seemed to take pride in giving Maverick a tour of the land that his new boss had bought. Maverick was pretty sure that Luke had ridden over this range several times.

He suspected that the boy had even had his own eye on it and was trying to figure out how to arrange to buy it.

"If you decide to work for me, Luke, and you prove yourself, I might stake you to some land of your own. A good place to start a family if you prove it up," Maverick told him.

"You'd do that for me?"

"I'd do it for Emma. You'll have to work hard and ride for the brand come hell or high water, Luke."

"I can sure do that, Mister Maverick," Luke replied.

"Just Maverick. Ain't no need for the mister."

"Yes, Sir." Luke told him.

"You know of any other hands in the area looking for work that are willing to ride for the brand?" Maverick asked.

"Yes, Sir, I surely do," Luke replied.

"They got experience working both cattle and horses?"

"Yes, they do."

"Good. I need good men. I'll tell you up front, we're going to have trouble with Silas Marcum when he finds out about it."

"He's an asshole," Luke replied.

"Agreed. But he also has the range that butts up against mine. Which means he ain't going to be happy about it, especially since I bum rushed him out of the café in front of the whole town," Maverick told him.

"I reckon you're reading that particular track right," Luke agreed.

"You know I am. So, are you willing to buck those kinds of odds?"

"You hired me, so I ride for the Maverick brand," Luke replied with a grin.

"In that case, where would you recommend that I build my ranch house?"

"I know just the place," Luke grinned, urging his horse forward. Maverick followed. Luke led him to an isolated glade next to a large pond. There were plenty of trees around to get lumber to build a log cabin. Maverick stepped down and outlined where he wanted the main cabin to sit as well as a barn and a couple of outbuildings.

"It looks to me that you have a sharp set of plans, Maverick," Luke told him.

"I try to, Luke. I want nothing more than to raise horses and cattle and have a good life doing so. I don't want trouble with my neighbors, but I damn well won't put up with any nonsense." Maverick told him.

"So, what do you want to do first?" Luke asked.

"I want to lay out my cabin and then we start finding flat stones to make a foundation," Maverick told him.

Marshal Woodrow stood in front of the door to his office looking out over the town. It was quiet enough as most folks were busy digging out from the storm. Horse traffic had pretty much pounded the snow in the street into a muddy slush that clung to the books unless you stuck to the boardwalks. A couple of stray dogs ran yipping down the street in pursuit of children enjoying a rare day out of school.

This was the Boulder that he liked to see, but he had bad feeling things wouldn't remain this quiet for long. Silas Marcum wouldn't take the shellacking that Maverick had given him lying down. Nor would he be happy when he discovered that Maverick had bought up a goodly portion of land that bordered his own.

No, trouble was coming to Boulder, one way or another. He could feel it in his bones. But was it from Marcum or someone else? He wished he knew. Personally, he would like nothing better than to toss Silas Marcum in the hoosegow and leave him there to rot. Nobody in town other that Levi Gorman, the banker, even liked the man. And truth be told, Woodrow had a feeling that Levi liked Marcum's money far more than he liked the man.

Woodrow decided to head over to the café for some coffee and maybe a spot of lunch. It was near enough to midday so taking his noon meal would be acceptable.

~ ~ ~

Natasha Ingle stood at the front window of her sewing shop. She was wondering about the man called Maverick. She had been present in the café when he had tossed Silas Marcum out into the street. He was a handsome man, and she was a single woman. She wondered how she might be able to meet him.

~ ~ ~

Maverick and Luke had spent the day gathering stones and setting them down and chinking them with mud inside the stakes and lines that Maverick had laid out. It had been back-breaking work, but young Luke had proven himself game. He had worked alongside Maverick without complaint. Maverick liked the kid. He had sand in him, more than a lot of boys his age. But Luke was just the start.

He needed to find some men, men that would ride for the brand regardless of the situation. He had a feeling that he could find some in Boulder. Most likely, they would have grudges against Silas Marcum for one reason or another. Marcum struck him as a man who threw a wide loop and didn't much care who he buffaloed to get what he wanted. What Maverick wanted, was some of the men that he had buffaloed. They would have the grit to stand against him as well as good reason.

Chapter 14

It was close to sunset when Maverick and Luke rode back into town. They headed straight to the café. It had been a long day and they were both tired and hungry. But the foundation had been laid for Maverick's house on his newly purchased property. Both men tied their horses at the hitching rail and went inside.

Macy greeted them both warmly before showing them to a table near the kitchen. She filled their coffee cups, gave them the day's specials, and then carried their orders into the back. Maverick leaned back in his chair as he sipped the hot coffee, letting it burrow deep into his insides.

The coffee warmed him after a long day spent out in the cold. He liked young Luke, and he hoped that the boy would help him find plenty of other young men willing to ride for the brand if treated well and paid a fair wage.

"About those other men you told me about, are you sure they would be willing to ride for brand and not cut and run at the first sight of trouble?" Maverick asked.

"I know some boys like that," Luke nodded.

"We need to get the ranch built first, and a barn and corral. I've got a man willing to sell me some cattle and some horses. But I want a place to work from first."

"That makes sense. Hank Clark is a good man with building things, and he's a steady hand with horses and cattle both. Poke Murray is solid and has plenty of guts. Dick Granger and Fred Tuttle are good men too. How much are you willing to pay?" Luke asked.

"Forty a month and found," Maverick replied.

"Them's fighting wages," Luke looked at him.

"They are. I suspect we'll have some fighting to do with Silas Marcum's crowd once he finds out I'm going into business next door."

"Boy howdy, ain't that the truth," Luke sighed. "Now I understand why you want men that are tough. How many hands do you want?"

"I figure about a dozen plus us, and I need a cook, preferably a trail cook that is used to working under harsh conditions and willing to pick up a gun if need be," Maverick replied.

"I think I know just the man for you. I'll have to ride up into the mountains to find him though, 'cause Charlie Grimsby is something of a loner. But you won't find a finer cook than Macy or Miss Emma unless it's Charlie," Luke told him.

"Does he like Marcum?" Maverick asked.

"Charlie hates him for all he's worth. Marcum fired him from the Barrel M when he took over. Most of the regular hands that were working there left after that and Marcum started hiring men of questionable backgrounds. They are a bunch bullies and like to run roughshod over most the folks in town," Luke explained.

"That's interesting."

"What do you know about Silas Marcum, Luke?" Maverick asked.

"Not a lot, really. He rode in a couple of years ago and bought the Barrel M off of Joe Morton. In a month he fired Charlie and most of the other hands and brought in his own crew to run things. His foreman is a gunman named Ben Carew, and he's said to be a fast man with a gun, but I've never personally seen him in a fight," Luke replied.

"Ben Carew. That name sounds familiar, but I just can't remember," Maverick said, his brow furrowing.

"You know him? Luke asked.

"I don't know, Luke and that's the truth. I lost my memories a little while back. My first memories are waking up in the middle of a slaughtered wagon train. I took the name Maverick because I really don't know who I am," Maverick admitted.

Macy reappeared with their food and refilled their coffee cups. Luke waited until she was gone before saying anything else. "That's quite a story, Boss," Luke said.

"Every word of it's true, Luke. All I can remember about my past is that there were men hunting me to try and kill me, but I have no idea who or why. But the name of Ben Carew rings a bell. I just don't know how or why," Maverick admitted.

"Do you think he might have been one of the men sent after you?" Luke asked.

"He might have been. I'm not one to run from trouble, Luke. If it comes, I'll meet it head on. I wouldn't ask any less for the men working for me. Nor would I hide behind them." Luke looked at him for a long moment, taking his measurement.

"I believe you, Boss. I'll round you up a good crew. You're paying more than a fair wage," Luke said. The two of them dug into their meal. Once his plate was cleaned, Luke headed off to start hiring men and left Maverick enjoying a third cup of coffee.

~ ~ ~

Natasha Ingle made her way to the café. She had seen Maverick and Luke Cantrell ride in. She had a feeling that they would head for the café for a bite to eat given that it was around the dinner hour. She wanted a good up-close look at this Maverick fellow. She was after all, a single woman in a western town. She had plenty of suitors, but none of them really interested her. Maverick was something of a mystery, and that intrigued her. She reached the café and pushed her way inside.

Though the café was busy, it didn't take her long to spot Maverick and make her way to his table. Maverick looked up at her. "Ma'am?" he asked.

"Hello, Mister Maverick. My name is Natasha Ingle. I'm the local seamstress in town," She introduced herself.

"The pleasure is mine, Miss Ingle, though I can't recall asking for your services," Maverick replied with a grin.

"You didn't. I was here the other day when you set Silas Marcum down a peg. I wanted to say thank you on behalf of the town folk," she replied.

"I take it you don't much care for Marcum?"

"You would be correct in your surmise," she admitted.

"So, what does that have to do with me?"

"I want to know more about you, Mister Maverick. I want to know what kind of man does that."

"I'm just a regular cowboy, Miss Ingle. Nothing more."

"Somehow, I doubt that, Mister Maverick."

"Why is that, Miss Ingle?"

"Because you are a man of action, Mister Maverick. You aren't one to let others run over you," she replied.

"And you know this how?" he asked.

"Because I study men, Mister Maverick." she told him.

"Why would you do that, Miss Ingle?" he asked.

"I am a woman, Mister Maverick, and as such, I look for a man that might make a suitable husband, Sir."

"Then you are looking in the wrong place, Miss Ingle. Because I am not at this time looking for a wife and if I were, I already have one in mind," Maverick told her. He stood and walked to the cash register to pay his bill. Natasha Ingle watched him go, her mouth hanging open, shocked that he had turned her down without so much as a second glance.

She sat there and fumed for a few minutes before paying for her coffee and stalking back up the snow-covered street toward her shop. Macy had walked to the window and watched her go, hiding a smile. She had never liked Miss Ingle. And while Maverick was too old for her, she had an idea of one of the women in town that he might fancy.

~ ~ ~

Roger Colton sat across from Oscar Bane. There was a bottle between them on the table and a full shot-glass sat in front of each man. They were in a far corner of the saloon well away from anyone else. The piano player was playing loudly on the far end of the room. There was no danger of them being overheard.

"You were looking for me, Mister Bane. Now, I'm here. What can I do for you?" Colton asked, reaching for his drink with his left hand. He was careful that way. His right hand remained out of sight under the table, the thong off the hammer of his Colt Peacemaker. He knew that Bane had taken notice of it as well. Bane made sure that he kept both of his hands in sight on top of the table. He reached for his glass as well.

"There's a man I want you to kill. It won't be easy," Bane said, as he tossed back his shot. He reached for the bottle and poured himself another.

"Who is it?" Colton asked, his curiosity be piqued.

"Out here, he's going by the name of Maverick. But you know him by another name," Bane said, turning his shot glass around on the table.

"What name do I know him by?"

"Gerald Kilburn," Bane said, softly.

"What?" Colton demanded, keeping his voice low enough to not draw attention.

"Of course, I remember. I killed him in Charleston near the end of the war," Colton said.

"Except he didn't die. I almost got him in Boston, and then again in Kentucky. I thought I had him on a wagon train heading west, but somehow the bastard managed to survive. He killed the men I sent after him again and again. So, I decided to send the best. Even though you managed not to kill him the last time you two faced off against each other," Bane tossed back his second shot and then pulled out a cigar, bit the end off of it and tucked it into his mouth and struck a match, drawing the flame inside as he twisted it around, making sure that he had it well lit.

"How do you know that Kilburn and this Maverick fellow are the same person?" Colton asked.

"Eye witness descriptions. Plus, I had that grave dug up down in Charleston. It was empty," Bane said, his tone smug.

"You know where this Maverick fellow is?" Colton asked. He was clearly irritated by the situation.

"Last word I heard, he was heading for Denver City and the Rockies, looking for some land to take up ranching," Bane said, softly.

"I'll find him. Me and Kilburn have some business between us to be settled," Colton growled.

"Just remember, he ain't going by Kilburn no more. He's calling himself Maverick these days."

"I'll remember," he said, standing up. He glared at Bane.

"You should have contacted me sooner," Colton said, before spinning on his heel and leaving. Bane watched him go.

Bane poured himself another drink and tossed it back. He hoped that Colton would be more successful than the others had been. Otherwise, he would have to face Kilburn down himself. He thought that he could take the man, but there was still that little tickle of uncertainty. It irritated him. Bane was not a man who liked fear. There was no mistaking the fact that he did fear Gerald Kilburn, no matter what the man was calling himself. Kilburn was a fighter and a killer. Bane took the bottle with him as he headed back to his room.

Luke made sure that he made plenty of noise as he approached Charlie Grimsby's place. Charlie was not a man that you wanted to sneak up on. Despite his age, he was almighty sudden with his six-gun, and if he grabbed a rifle or shotgun, nobody stood a chance against him. Luke had known Charlie for many years and he just hoped that the old man still recognized him. If Maverick wanted Charlie for a cook, there was nobody better, be it on the ranch or on a chuckwagon for a drive.

"Hello, Charlie!" he called out loudly as he approached the gate. He stopped his horse and called again.

"Climb down and come on in, but close the gate behind you," a gravelly voice called from the shadows.

"Yes, Sir, Charlie. It's me, Luke Cantrell. I came to offer you a job," Luke called out. He hoped that the old man would remember him and not shoot him.

"Keep your hands where I can see 'em boy. You reach for a gun and I'll spread your innards all over the yard," Charlie's voice called back.

"Ain't no need for that Charlie. I ain't here for no trouble."

"Well, if'n you is, you done found a bushel of it!" Charlie replied.

"Charlie, it's me, Luke Cantrell. You remember me don't ya?" Luke called.

"Luke, is that you?" Charlie asked.

"It is, Charlie," Luke replied.

"Well why didn't you say so right off the bat?" Charlie demanded, appearing out of the shadows.

"I did, Charlie. I just figured you didn't hear me," Luke told him.

"What the hell are you doing all the way out here, Boy?"

"I came to offer you a job, Charlie," Luke told him.

Chapter 15

"That's some story, Luke. You figure that this fella Maverick is on the up and up?" Charlie asked.

"He stood up to Silas Marcum and tossed him out of the café after Marcum had made Miss Macy cry. Plus, he showed me the bill of sale for the land he bought. We spent the day putting in a foundation for his house on his spread. He's offering forty a month and found for anybody willing to ride for the brand," Luke explained.

"He's expecting trouble from Marcum and his gang then?"

"He is."

"Well count me in, Luke. You want to bunk here for the night, and then I'll ride back down the mountain with you in the morning?" Charlie asked.

"I'd appreciate it Charlie. I'm plumb worn out," Luke agreed.

~ ~ ~

"That was some show you put on over at the café last night," Gideon Shade commented as Maverick entered the saloon. Jonathan was busy pouring drinks as Maverick took a seat at Shade's table. The man was dealing solitaire to himself again.

"Heard about that, did you?" Maverick asked, taking a chair across from him.

"Everybody in town heard," Shade grinned at him.

"People talk too much."

"Maybe so, Maverick, but you're a man to take notice of now. Nobody else around here had the fortitude to stand up to Silas Marcum, not even Marshal Woodrow."

"That's funny, Woodrow backed my play last night. He may have more guts than you give him credit for," Maverick told him.

"That he might," Shade nodded.

"Looks like you're having trouble scrounging up a game," Maverick observed.

"Mostly just townsfolk around now. Miners won't be in until the weekend. That's when there will be money to be made," Shade replied, nonchalantly.

"For you, maybe. I got a feeling that the miners don't fare as well."

"That is in the hands of Lady Luck, Maverick. I'm good enough I don't need to cheat. Sometimes I win, sometimes I lose. It all comes down to the luck of the draw," Shade shrugged.

"I believe you," Maverick said, standing and heading upstairs to his room. Maverick could have moved over to the hotel, but he liked the room over the saloon. It was quiet enough to suit him, and Blocker and Shade made sure that he wasn't disturbed. Most men figured it just wouldn't be worth it.

Besides, with luck, he'd be moving into his new ranch house in a month or two. Of course, all of his hands would be bunking with him until they got a bunkhouse built as well. He had a good feeling about the men that Luke had told him about. They sounded like a salty bunch, and that was what he would need to stand against Silas Marcum and his men. Maverick knew that he wouldn't be able to do it on his own.

~ ~ ~

Lilly Cambridge was surprised to hear a knock on her door at such a late hour. She snatched up one of the .36 Navy Colt's that had been converted to cartridges and carried it in her right hand as she approached the door. "Who is it?" Lilly called, her thumb on the hammer and ready to cock it back.

"It's Macy, Miss Lilly," called a voice she knew well. Lilly opened the door and let Macy inside, bolting the door behind her.

"Why are you here so late, Macy?" Lilly asked.

"I have some news for you, Miss Lilly," Macy told her primly.

"What sort of news would that be, Macy?" Lilly asked.

"There's a new man in town, Lilly."

"Now, why would I care about that?"

"Because he beat Silas Marcum down and tossed him out of the café after Marcum made me cry. And, he sent Miss Ingle packing after she had her sights set on him," Macy replied.

"He certainly sounds like a man of good breeding," Lilly smiled at Macy.

"Of that he is, and I can testify it myself. Silas insulted me and Emma, and Maverick came to our defense. He tossed him out into the snow and Marshal Woodrow even backed him up!" Macy explained.

"Now, that is a sight I wish I could have seen. Marshal Woodrow has done little when it comes to standing up to Silas Marcum."

"Come to the café tomorrow for breakfast and I'll introduce you," Macy told her.

"I can do that," Lilly confirmed.

"I was hoping that you might," Macy told her. Then Macy hurried out the door, heading back to the café where she and Emma shared quarters.

Lilly watched her go, keeping an eye on her until she reached the stand of buildings where the café was located. This Maverick fellow sounded interesting to her. It had been a long time since any man had tickled her fancy.

~ ~ ~

Macy walked quickly towards the buildings where her café was located. The air had grown colder with sundown and clear skies. Even the slight breeze of her walking made her face burn with cold. It would be interesting setting up Miss Lilly and Maverick. She had a feeling that they would find one another interesting enough to pursue something. She had just reached the edge of the buildings when she heard footsteps crunching in the snow of the alley that she had to pass to reach Main Street. She knew better than to walk at night alone even in their fair town of Boulder.

Her heartbeat quickened as she swung out to the opposite side of the street in order to pass the alley. A man's voice called out to her, but Macy kept going, breaking into a run to get away from the edge of town and down Main Street. She could hear heavy footsteps behind her as the man ran to catch her. She glanced back over her shoulder, but it was too dark to see his face. Macy screamed as loud as she could as she ran. The marshal stepped out of his office and onto the boardwalk, a rifle in his hands. Macy heard a snarled curse from behind her as the man that had been chasing her darted between two buildings.

Marshal Woodrow cautiously made his way to her, his eyes roaming the street. Macy collapsed into his arms. Men had come out of the saloon and a couple of them came over to help the marshal get Macy to his office. Once he had her sitting down, he gave her a cup of coffee with some whiskey in it to calm her nerves. Macy was just starting to calm down when Maverick came through the door. Macy seemed to take some comfort from seeing him there. "Macy, what happened?" he asked softly, kneeling before her.

"I was on my way home from Miss Cambridge's house and I heard someone in the alley at the edge of town. I circled out away from the buildings and started running up Main Street. Whoever it was started chasing me. I could hear him closing in behind me and I started screaming. As soon as the marshal stepped outside, whoever it was, darted in between some buildings," Macy told it just how it happened.

"There was somebody chasing her all right. I could see their outline against the snow, but he was too far away for me to identify," Marshal Woodrow added.

"Marshal, if you'll see Miss Macy home, I'm going to go look and see if I can find that varmint's tracks," Maverick said coldly. Woodrow looked up at him and nodded. The men from the saloon that had followed Maverick from the bar went with him, a couple carrying kerosene lanterns.

Maverick took one of the lamps and led the way. He had slipped the hammer thong off of his Colt Russian .44 so he could bring it into play quicker. He found the alley where Macy's pursuer had turned off the main street and darted down and alley. Maverick's eyes narrowed as he studied the tracks in the snow, memorizing everything about the track. If he ever saw those tracks again, he would recognize them. And he planned to kill the man wearing them if he found him. Macy didn't deserve being scared like she was tonight.

Maverick wondered if this had something to do with him tossing Silas Marcum out of the Miss Emma's Café the day before. Was Marcum that vindictive that he would take it out on the girls? Maverick felt that the answer was probably ... yes. Maverick and the men followed the tracks back to where a horse had been tied up. Maverick memorized those tracks as well. The man that had tried to hurt Macy was as good as dead, he just didn't know it yet.

Maverick headed back to Blocker's place which was rapidly emptying out. After the earlier excitement on the street, Jonathan had decided to close up early.

"What happened?" Gideon Shade asked Maverick as he entered.

"Some son of a bitch tried to attack Macy earlier," Maverick said, his anger evident in his tone.

"Whoever it was, they's a damn fool. Macy is well-liked around town," Shade replied.

"Once I find out who it was, he's a dead man."

"I can see that."

"Good night," Maverick said, heading up the stairs to his room. Gideon Shade watched him go. The gambler shook his head. He knew exactly how Maverick felt. Every man in town felt some kind of affection towards the gals that ran the café. Nobody had staked a claim on Macy as yet, but it wouldn't be long. She was a pretty young girl. But she hadn't deserved to be frightened like she was tonight. Given the chance, Gideon shade would gladly put a bullet into the man that had done it.

~ ~ ~

Artie Simms cursed as he rode away from town. He had almost had the girl that Silas Marcum wanted. But then the marshal had come outside and there was no way in hell that he was going to go to jail for the likes of Silas Marcum. Artie was one of the man gunslingers that Marcum had hired after his real cowhands had quit on him.

Ben Carew was the current *El Jefe Segundo* on the ranch, second in command, though he really didn't do much more than order the others around. Simms hated pushing cows, so he had jumped at this opportunity when it had been offered to him. Now, he had to go back and report that he had failed. It didn't sit well with him.

~ ~ ~

Charlie Grimsby had biscuits and gravy on the table when Luke rolled out of his blankets with the coming of morning. Charlie had already been up a good hour but had let him sleep knowing that there was going to be a lot of work ahead of everybody that Maverick hired. Both men dug into their breakfasts and ate quickly, making sure they had cleaned their plates. Luke helped Charlie clean up and then the two of them headed back down the mountain into town.

~ ~ ~

Lilly Cambridge stepped into 'Miss Emma's Café' early. The sun had barely crested the horizon, but she wanted to meet this Maverick fellow. Macy rushed up to her and showed her to a table at the back.

"What's wrong, Macy?" Lilly asked.

"A man tried to attack me on my way home from your place last night," Macy explained.

"Any idea who it was?" Lilly bristled.

"I wish I did, Miss Lilly. But I couldn't see his face. Mister Maverick went looking for him, but the man had ridden out of town."

"Bring me some biscuits and gravy and some coffee," Lilly ordered, her anger visible in her eyes.

"Yes, Ma'am," Macy quickly disappeared into the back. Macy bought her order quickly, and about that time was when Maverick strolled into the dining room. Macy smiled and waved as she made her way across the dining room to where he waited at the door.

"Mister Maverick, good morning!"

"Good morning, Macy. I wanted to see how you were feeling after your ordeal last night," Maverick greeted her.

"I'm feeling much better this morning. I never should have gone to the edge of town so late."

"Why were you out there anyways, sweetheart?"

"I went to talk to someone. There is somebody that I'd like you to meet. A friend of mine that I went to see," Macy said, taking his hand and guiding him across the room.

They stopped at a table occupied by a beautiful redhead. Her hair was pulled up in the fashionable knot with ringlets of red falling down her back. She was very striking in her rich dove grey silk skirt filled with petticoats and adorned by grey ribbons with a matching grey velour bodice with a grey velvet jacket. A black felt hat trimmed with a long grey feather complimented her beauty and framed her green eyes that glinted with humor.

"Mister Maverick, this is Miss Lilly Cambridge. She's a friend of mine and she is the owner of a couple of the smaller ranches that have been having trouble with Silas Marcum and the Barrel M," Macy said, by way of introduction.

"Miss Cambridge," Maverick looked into her eyes, smiled and bowed slightly, taking off his hat.

"The pleasure is mine, Mister Maverick," Lilly replied, a slight blush coming to her cheeks. Indeed, Maverick did cut a fine figure of a man with his wide shoulders, muscular chest and arms, and narrow hips.

"Not all of it, I hope, may I join you?" Maverick asked her, as he slid out a chair and took the seat opposite her.

Chapter 16

Luke Cantrell and Charlie Grimsby were on the trail back to town by sunrise. The wind was a light breeze, but it still had a bite to it thanks to the snow pack on the ground. It would take a couple of hours to get to town and they could warm up in the café. It would be good to spend a few minutes with Emma, Luke thought. It made him smile.

"How much trouble do you think this Maverick fellow is stepping into with Marcum?" Charlie asked.

"I'd guess quite a bit after tossing him out into the snow in front of half the town, and then buying up the land around the Barrel M and setting up his own ranch," Luke chuckled,

"It sure does sound like fun. Who else has Maverick got?"

"Just you and me so far, but I've yet to talk to Hank Clark, Poke Murray, Dick Granger and Fred Tuttle. I figured they'd be willing to buck Marcum," Luke said.

"I'll round up some of the boys that used to work for old Joe Morton when we get to town. None of those boys liked Marcum and they're a right salty bunch onc't riled up," Charlie chuckled.

"Ain't that the truth! I seen Paddy Morgan take on four men in a fist fight and walk off without being winded. You know where Paddy can be found?" Luke asked.

"Him, and a few others. Sounds like this Maverick is going to need all the help he can get!" Charlie said.

"Don't sell Maverick short, Charlie. I've seen him in action and he's hell on wheels in a fight. Let's get on to town. I've got me a hankerin' for a slice of Miss Emma's apple pie."

~ ~ ~

Lilly looked across the table at Maverick while she sipped her coffee. They had both finished their breakfast and were on their second cup. She had discovered that Maverick was a man of exceptional intelligence and charm, as well as being very well read for a man of the west. She had discovered something else as well. She liked this man who went by the name of Maverick.

"Macy mentioned that you own a couple of the smaller ranches in the area?" Maverick asked.

"I do. My late husband had purchased them before the gunman Carew gunned him down like a dog in the street without warning. Marcum has tried to run my people off, stopping just short of threatening me himself," Lilly explained.

"I don't much care for the man, but I'm starting to dislike him a whole lot more," Maverick said, his face a stone-like mask.

"I've been fighting him on my own for a while now, but Marcum has too much money backing him. But, I'd be willing to throw in with you, which would give you land on three sides of him," Lilly said.

"Are your men willing to fight and ride for the brand?" Maverick asked.

"They'll ride for me," Lilly said.

"Why?"

"Most of them were soldiers with my husband in the war. They were loyal to him, and after he was murdered, they became loyal to me."

"I believe that I fought for the Union as well, Mrs. Cambridge," Maverick told her.

"It's Miss Cambridge now. It has been ever since Jeremiah was killed, and please, call me Lilly."

"Well, be that as it may, Miss Lilly, you've got yourself a partner in this. I've sent Luke Cantrell to round up some hands to help me build my ranch house and a barn and corrals and a bunkhouse. I've got a man in Texas willing to sell me about a thousand head of longhorns and fifty head of horses, but I need to have a base of operations first. I've already registered my brand, that of a long-horned cow as the Maverick brand," he explained.

"I'll lend you men to help build, Mister Maverick. They'll be prepared to fight as well if need be," Lilly told him.

"Then we have a deal and please, call me Maverick," he told her. They shook hands.

"May I ride out and see your place?" Lilly asked.

"It would be a pleasure to show it to you, Miss Lilly, but there ain't all that much to see as of yet," Maverick told her.

"Seeing how a man plans to live can tell a woman a lot about him, Maverick," Lilly favored him with a dazzling smile.

"I'm sure it can. But I'd rather wait until we have a full crew of hands to ride with us. I'm right cautious that way."

"That is a good trait for a business man, Maverick."

"So, I've been told," he smiled at her, draining his cup.

~ ~ ~

Marshal Woodrow was concerned. Maverick had stopped by and told him what he and the others had found the night before on his way to the café. Somebody had been lying in wait for Macy. Somebody that meant to do her harm. He didn't like that. Didn't like it at all. One of the unwritten rules of the west was that no man would hurt a woman, not unless he wanted to hang. Shooting a man was one thing, but harming a woman? That took a real animal to do something like that. There were far more men in the west than women and as such, women were considered as a treasure more valuable than gold. So, if somebody had been lying in wait for Miss Macy, they were lower than a snake's belly and he wouldn't hesitate to shoot them down like a dog if they were to try it again.

~ ~ ~

"I don't like what went on out there last night," Jonathan Blocker said, as he wiped down the bar. It was early morning and he and Gideon Shade were the only ones present in the saloon.

"I don't either, Jonathan. Attacking that poor little girl? That was the work of an animal, not a man," Shade replied, as he shuffled the pasteboards in his hand and dealt them out on the tabletop.

"Trouble is coming Gideon. I can feel it in my bones," Blocker said softly.

"I knew that as soon as Maverick arrived, my friend. He draws trouble like a lightning rod draws lightning."

"Maybe so, but I like him."

"So, do I, Jonathan. So, do I." Gideon replied.

"So, how do you think we can help him out?"

"Have Buck Wilson run the bar and we keep an eye on them girls at the café to make sure that nobody bothers them when Maverick isn't around," Shade replied.

"I can do that. Buck's a good man and honest to. Plus, he's sudden enough with his six-shooter to stop any real trouble afore it gets started," he noted.

"He is at that," Shade agreed.

~ ~ ~

Charlie Grimsby followed Luke Cantrell into the café. He had eaten there a time or two when he was in town and had to grudgingly admit that Miss Emma and Miss Macy were damn near his equals in the kitchen. Luke spotted Maverick sitting and talking with Miss Lilly over coffee and led Charlie over to their table.

126

"Maverick, this here is Charlie Grimsby, the cook I told you about," Luke said by way of introduction. He had taken his hat off as they approached the table and held it in his hands.

"Mister Grimsby, I'm Maverick," he said standing and shaking hands with the cook.

"Nice to meet you, Maverick. Miss Cambridge," Charlie acknowledged, shaking hands.

"Charlie, it's been a while. How have you been?" Lilly asked.

"Just fine, Miss Lilly. I was right sorry to hear about Mister Cambridge. He was a good man."

"He was, Charlie. I miss him every day. But I want you to know, I'm throwing in with Maverick here."

"That's surely gonna put a burr under old Marcum's saddle," Charlie chuckled.

"I certainly hope so," Lilly laughed as well.

"Boss, if it's alright with you, I'm gonna take a few minutes to pay call on Miss Emma before I go round up the rest of those men I told you about," Luke said.

"Go ahead," Maverick told him with a smile. He knew the young man had a case for Miss Emma and he was not one to stand in the way of young love. Macy appeared at their table again with a full pot of coffee.

"Hey, Charlie. You want some coffee?" Macy asked.

"Sure do, Miss Macy. I reckon the Boss and Miss Lilly can use a refill as well," Charlie told her. Macy filled their cups before looking at Maverick.

"Charlie is almost as good a cook as Emma, Mister Maverick, you won't go wrong with him," she said.

"Almost! Why, young lady, do I need to turn you over my knee, knocking your betters that way?" Charlie exclaimed.

"I suspect you'd have to go through both Mister Maverick and Miss Cambridge for that," Macy replied sweetly, then she sashayed off.

"She's right, Charlie," Maverick said quietly. Charlie opened his mouth and closed it three times before adopting a sheepish expression.

"I reckon so, and I ain't about to blow a chance to get in Marcum's face," Charlie chuckled. "You'll do, Maverick. You'll do." Maverick smiled at him.

~ ~ ~

Jimmy Rogers rode into Boulder. It had become a boom town, and it was close enough to the mines to stay alive longer than most. He was right hungry and after he filled his belly, he'd ride on to the Barrel M and give Mister Marcum the proposal from Major Carr. Jimmy had a feeling that Marcum would be receptive. He had been sympathetic to The South when Jimmy had ridden off to join the Confederate Army. He rode to the livery to get his horse some grain and warmed up as well.

~ ~ ~

Silas Marcum was still angry over what had happened the other night. He was also pissed that Artie had failed to hurt the girl that ran the café. Ben Carew had entered the room. And stood waiting on the other side of his desk. "You wanted to see me, Boss?" Carew asked, laconically.

"I do, Ben. Have a seat," Marcum ordered. Carew sat down in the chair across from the desk.

"So, what's up, Boss?"

"There is a man in town causing me trouble. He says his name is Maverick," Marcum explained.

"Maverick?" Carew looked at him, puzzled.

"You ever heard of him?"

"I can't say that I have, Boss."

Chapter 17

Silas Marcum was surprised to hear the knock on his front door. Usually, his men just walked in unannounced if they needed to talk to him. He got up and walked to the door, throwing it open. "Jimmy?" he exclaimed in shock. He hadn't seen Jimmy Rogers since he had rode off to fight for the Confederacy. Now, here the boy stood, still wearing the gray.

"Mister Marcum, Sir. I was hoping we might talk for a bit," Jimmy said, his teeth chattering with cold.

"Certainly, Jimmy come on in and get warm," Marcum said, stepping out of the way. Marcum rang a bell and his cook entered the room. "Bring this man some hot coffee and some food," Marcum commanded.

Marcum ushered Jimmy to a chair. "What brings you back this way, Jimmy?" Marcum asked.

"Well, I've still been riding with Major Carr since the war ended, he's my commanding officer, and he was wondering if we could lay up here and rest for a few days before heading on down to Old Mexico."

"I'm sympathetic to your cause, Jimmy. How many men?"" Marcum asked, wheels turning in his head.

"About a dozen, Mister Marcum." Jimmy went quiet, as the cook returned with two cups of coffee on a tray and a plate with sliced beef sandwiches. Marcum took one cup and Jimmy took the other plus the plate with the sandwiches on it. The boy ate like he was starving. Marcum sipped his coffee as he began thinking how he could turn Jimmy and his rebel friends to his advantage.

~ ~ ~

Ben Carew rode into Boulder. He figured from what Marcum had told him that he would find

Maverick at 'Miss Emma's Café'. It appeared that he set some store by the two girls that ran it, and Artie had blown his chance of grabbing one of them the night before. To hell with making it look like an accident, he planned on killing Maverick straight up. Carew was a big brute of a man with bulging muscles, a thick black beard, and as nasty a disposition as a sore toothed grizzly. He'd never been beaten with fists or guns. And he was in a right mood to beat Maverick to death with his bare hands. Carew hated riding out in the cold, and even though the storm had blown through, but the bitter cold remained, and it chilled him to the bone. One thing that he had never liked was being cold. He had worked long and hard to pack on muscle, hoping it would help, and it had. He tied his horse off at the rail in front of the café, not caring if the animal got cold or not, and stomped his way up onto the boardwalk and pushed his way inside.

~ ~ ~

"Maverick!" Lilly Cambridge grasped his wrist tightly, as she saw the big man enter.

"What is it, Lilly?" Maverick asked, picking up on her concern. Her face had gone pale as well.

"The man that just came in, that's Ben Carew. The man that killed my husband for Marcum," Lilly said in a near whisper. Maverick's eyes narrowed as he looked at the near giant. Maverick stood up, slipping a pair of tight leather gloves on his hands.

"I'm looking for the man calling himself Maverick!" Ben Carew said loudly. All conversation in the café stopped.

"I'm Maverick," he said, walking towards the man.

"Good. I'm going to kill you," Carew said, with a sadistic smile.

"If you want to fight, let's take it outside," Maverick told him.

"Why should I?" Carew asked.

"Because I asked nicely," Maverick smiled, before delivering a haymaker that drove the larger man back towards the door. A quick-thinking townsman threw the door wide, as Maverick hit Carew again and sent him stumbling back outside. Ben Carew fell off the boardwalk and landed on his ass in the street. Ben Carew shook his head as he climbed to his feet. He touched his smashed lips and his hand came away bloody. He looked at Maverick.

"I don't like being hit, Mister," Carew growled.

"You asked for it, Carew, when you asked for me," Maverick said.

"Like hell," Carew spat blood and then he charged Maverick. Maverick side-stepped him and hooked a right into his stomach that folded the big man in half. Maverick slammed his elbow down on Carew's neck, dropping the big man to the ground.

Carew forced himself up to his knees, and then staggered to his feet. His face was a bloody mess. He charged Maverick and threw his arms wide, grabbing Maverick up in a massive bear hug, squeezing his arms tightly together. Maverick slapped his gloved hands against the man's ears, rupturing his eardrums. Maverick drove his elbow against the man's nose, cracking the bone, and then slammed his palm against it, driving the bone back up into the brain. Ben Carew went limp as he died, and Maverick rolled free of his embrace.

~ ~ ~

Maverick stood over the man, panting and gasping for air. Carew had been a man to fight for sure. Marshal Woodrow came running down the street. He took in Maverick's torn shirt and the dead body laying at his feet. He looked at the dead man's face. Then he looked at Maverick. "That's Ben Carew," Woodrow said.

"I heard that already," Maverick told him.

"I bet you did," Woodrow sighed.

"Carew come in looking for him, Marshal," Dude Yancy said. I heard Carew call him out."

"So did I," Harvey Pettigrew added.

"Me too, Marshal," Gloria Cain added.

"Then I reckon it was self-defense. Dude, run down the street and tell Potter you've a client for him. I just to figure out how I'm going to tell Marcum that his *Segundo* is dead without a shot being fired," Woodrow said.

"I reckon I can deliver that message personal, Marshal," Maverick offered with a grin.

"I can't help but think that is a right poor idea, Maverick. Are you sure you want to settle around here?"

"I've already bought land that butts up against the Barrel M spread, Marshal. Me and the boys are going to get my house built and a bunkhouse, barn, and corrals here in the next few days. Miss Cambridge has offered me some men to help with that as well, since the Barrel M has been targeting her two spreads as well," Maverick said, smiling at the Marshal's discomfort.

"Oh, Lordy," Marshal Woodrow groaned. Because he knew most of the old boys that rode for Lilly Cambridge and they were a right salty tough bunch, "Just try to keep the trouble out of town."

"How about you making sure that Miss Macy and Miss Emma are well protected after they close up?" Maverick asked in reply.

"I'll do as best I can," Woodrow sighed. He turned and headed back up the street towards his office.

"That was an impressive display of fisticuffs, Maverick," Lilly Cambridge said admiringly, as he stepped back up onto the boardwalk.

"He had no manners, Miss Lilly," Maverick replied, stripping the gloves off his hands and tucking them into his back pocket, as he walked back inside. Macy ran to him.

"Are you hurt, Mister Maverick?" she gasped.

"Not so's you'd notice, Macy. But I'd be obliged if you would get me a pan of hot water that I can soak my hands in so that they don't swell," Maverick told her.

"You have a seat and I'll be right out with it," Macy told him. Maverick walked back to the table, followed by Lilly Cambridge.

~ ~ ~

The undertaker, Otto Potter, had brought his wagon upon learning that Ben Carew was dead. He had also purchased the help of two strong men to load Carew into his wagon and to lift him into a plain wood coffin when they got back to his shop. Ben Carew was not a well-liked man in Boulder. Perhaps, even less well-liked than his boss Silas Marcum. Potter sent a rider heading for the Barrel M to let Marcum know that Carew was dead. He knew that Marcum would pay for the man's burial.

~ ~ ~

Jimmy was back on the trail, carrying the news that Marcum had agreed to let the troops stay there for a couple of weeks. Marcum was still sympathetic to The South. He hoped that Major Carr would be pleased. He suspected that Carr and Marcum would hit it off just fine.

~ ~ ~

Lilly Cambridge regarded the man she knew as Maverick through new eyes. Not only was he handsome, but strong and determined as well. He had whipped Ben Carew to death as if it were nothing. And then he had joked with the Marshal about it. He was a man like her late husband, a man to ride the river with.

Whatever happened, she planned on getting to know Maverick very well over the next few months. He was a fine-looking man, and Boulder, lively as it was a lonely enough place for a widow woman, even a wealthy one like her. She couldn't help but wonder what it might feel like to have his strong arms wrapped around her. Or what his kisses might taste like? That was something that she wanted to find out on her own, and sooner rather than later. Lilly wished that they served whiskey in the café, for at the moment, she could surely use a drink.

~ ~ ~

Luke came back to the café with Hank Clark, Poke Murray, Dick Granger and Fred Tuttle in tow. After hearing what Maverick had planned, they quickly agreed to sign on with him. Charlie returned with several hands that had worked for Joe Morton, including Kiowa Joe, Ding Bartell, Quinn Summers, Jake Bean, Mark Costa, and Harvey Kingman. None of them cared for Silas Marcum and would as soon shoot him as listen to him.

"You know that we'll be going up against Silas Marcum and his boys, right?" Maverick asked.

"That don't make no shakes with us," Ding Bartell replied. Ding was a sorrowful-looking man that looked like nothing could make him smile. The truth was, the worse things looked against him, the happier Ding was.

"Then I expect to see you all at the livery within the hour. We'll have to work the rest of the day and start again at sunrise. Charlie Grimsby is picking up supplies to start cooking at the ranch. Miss Lilly is going to send riders up to help tomorrow, so stay sharp tonight," Maverick told them. The men nodded and left the café.

"You're doing the right thing, Maverick. Each and every one of those men will ride for the brand and follow you through the gates of hell. Are you sure that you want to take on Silas Marcum?" Lilly asked him.

"I am. I'm also hoping that you'll be neighborly and come around to visit some," Maverick winked at her.

"I'm sure that I can," Lilly told him.

~ ~ ~

Jonas Carr was growing impatient at the mining camp. They had been waiting there nigh unto a week. What was taking Jimmy so long? If they had to wait too much longer, he would just cut his men loose and they would murder and rob their way to the Mexican border. He was thinking about the town of Boulder. It was a mining town. A boom town as it were. It was a place where miners cashed in their gold for currency. It was also a place where they gambled away a lot of their money. It might be worth raiding before they headed for the Barrel M. It was something that Carr would have to think about.

~ ~ ~

Silas Marcum had been impressed with Jimmy's plan. It would, in fact, give him extra men to deal with Maverick if Ben Carew failed in his task to kill the man. He suspected that Jonas Carr was less worried about rearming The South than covering his own ass. It was something that Marcum had seen more than once. Having a company of rebels kill off Maverick would certainly ease his difficulties with the man. Marcum smiled at the thought. He shook his head as his daughter rode off into the snow storm that was currently blanketing the heights of the Rockies.

Chapter 18

Miss Lilly had gone back to her place by the time Luke came back with the crew. Maverick fed them all and then they went over to the general store to make sure each man had warm clothes and serviceable weapons. He also purchased half a dozen axes. Hank Clark had arrived with a wagon full of tools. Maverick bought plenty of provisions, animal hides for warm covering and heavy-duty canvas tents for the hands to stay in until they had a structure ready to hold them. The way Maverick saw it he could get by with dirt floors until spring. Once warm weather arrived, he could put a wood floor in.

He knew that most of the folks in town thought that he was crazy to go after Silas Marcum, bucking him to the point of building his ranch right next to Marcum's. What they didn't understand, was that he hated bullies of all stripes. And Silas Marcum was nothing more than a coward and a bully. He was the type that had his killing done for him because he didn't have the guts to buckle on a gun and do it himself.

Several folks watched them ride out of town, and Maverick knew that he and his men would be the topics of many conversations around town later in the evening. It didn't matter much to him. It seemed like he had been running since before he had come to after the wagon train had been hit. Well, he had run long enough, and it was time to make a stand.

Trouble was going to find him no matter where he went. So, now he was ready to stand and face it once and for all. Running from trouble never allowed a man to rest. Facing it head on, that was the best way to deal with it.

It was late afternoon when they reached the spot that Maverick had elected to put his home. He had the men start pitching tents as Charlie built a cook fire and started supper. They wouldn't get much work done today, but they would be ready to start bright and early come morning.

~ ~ ~

Lilly Cambridge had sent word to Tyrell Oldham and Newt McCall, the foremen of her two spreads for them to come to her. She liked Maverick. He had a steadiness about him that she had found in few men besides her husband. It was clear that he was a man of breeding and intelligence. He reminded her of her husband in many ways, but he was unique in his own way. He had also made it quite clear that he liked her, as well. She smiled as she shook her head. Macy hadn't even been sneaky about her attempt at match making. That didn't bother her, not really. She liked Macy and knew that her heart was in the right place. It had been a few years, and Lilly was still a young woman. Having a man would keep her from shriveling up and wasting away, as had happened to many widows in the west. There had been a certain spark with Maverick that she hadn't felt for a long time.

~ ~ ~

Maverick was still working on the tall chimney for the fireplace when Luke walked up. The rest of the men were busy cutting down logs and hauling them in for the cabin walls that would soon be their base of operations.

"Boss?" Luke asked.

"What is it Luke?" Maverick asked.

"I've been doing some thinking. How would you feel about having the bunkhouse connected to the main house? That would certainly make it easier to defend," Luke suggested.

"That sounds like a good idea to me, Luke. You want to start finding some foundation stones?" Maverick asked him.

"There's plenty of them about. I'll have Fred Tuttle help me with that," Luke nodded.

"Then git to it without taking up my time from building this chimney," Maverick told him. Luke took off, leaving Maverick to smile. Luke's suggestion was something that he had already thought of, but he wanted the young man to think of on his own.

Maverick had the men pitch the largest tent inside the foundation near the fireplace and once he had it built up high enough, he started stacking wood inside the fireplace. After supper, he'd built the fire up enough to warm up the tent for the men that would be sleeping in it. Of course, they would never all be sleeping at once. Given his relationship with Marcum, Maverick figured it best to post guards. The others agreed with him. Charlie and Hank offered to take the first watch. Maverick agreed, and decided that he and Luke would take the final watch.

Charlie had boiled up some cowboy stew using some venison that Luke had shot on their way out to the ranch site. The stew was tasty and good and filling and they all went back for seconds which put a smile on Charlie's face despite him grousing that if they kept it up they'd need another deer shot tomorrow in order to have enough food.

~ ~ ~

Silas Marcum was cussing a blue streak after listening to the word that Nick French had brought him about Ben Carew. It shocked him to find out that Maverick had managed to kill the big man with his fists. Nobody had ever beaten Ben Carew in a fist fight.

"Who the hell is this Maverick?" Marcum demanded.

"Nobody seems to know much about him, Mister Marcum. He rode into town just after the blizzard hit," French supplied.

"Nobody had seen or heard of him before that?" Marcum asked.

"Not in Boulder, Mister Marcum," French replied.

"Somebody somewhere must know something about him," Marcum said thoughtfully.

"That sounds, reasonable," Nick agreed.

"Nick, I'm going to give you money to send some wires out. I want you to find out if anybody in Colorado knows anything about this man," Marcum told him.

"I'll do it, Mister Marcum," Nick told him. Marcum thrusts several greenbacks into his hands.

"Find out Nick. Find out as quick as you can," Marcum said. Nick French headed for the door. Marcum walked back to his sideboard and poured himself a glass full of whiskey. He took a sip and felt it burning its way down to his belly. Maverick, whoever the hell he was, was going to die.

~ ~ ~

Colton kept away from mining camps as he rode south along the river. He wanted no word spreading ahead of him that he was on the hunt. Colton was a known manhunter across the west. He didn't want this Maverick to know that he was after him. It was hard to think of Kilburn under this new name, but even Colton had to admit that it suited the man. Kilburn had been a well-respected officer in the Yankee Army. He had also been a man that was a tactical genius. He understood guerilla tactics better than anyone else in the Union Army! Kilburn was a fast hand with a gun as well. Colton had shot the man from ambush in Charleston, South Carolina. He was sure that he had killed him then, but it was evident that he hadn't. So, he owed Kilburn. Owed him a quick and painful death.

~ ~ ~

Lilly Cambridge poured herself a brandy in her boarding room. The men that she was sending would join Maverick in the morning to help with building up his place. Once that was done, she knew that he planned to send word to a rancher in Texas that he wanted to buy cattle. He had a good plan and the breeding of those longhorns with some of the local white-faced cows would be interesting.

She took a sip, enjoying the sensation as the warm liquor hit her stomach and began to spread warmth through her body. She got up and stoked the fire in the fireplace. She tossed on a couple of more pieces of wood and returned to her desk. She opened a drawer and pulled out a leather-bound journal. She had started keeping it when she had traveled west from Baltimore with her husband after the war. They had come to Colorado and had chosen to settle beneath the beautiful mountains, filing on different sections of land. They had gotten both of the ranches up and running and were doing well.

Her husband had recognized that Boulder was a boom town, one that had grown because of the discovery of gold and the mines and the incoming railroads. But the people were a better sort than most of those that moved from town to town until the mines played out. Many of the people of Boulder would stick things out, the people that had settled in Boulder were men and women who wanted to stay and make something of the town. Until Silas Marcum had arrived.

All anybody knew about him was that he was from back east and he had money. He had bought the Barrel M from Joe Morton and Joe had lit a shuck for back east. At least that's what Silas had claimed. Nobody, including the men that had worked for Joe Morton had seen him sign the bill of sale or seen him leave. Joe had just disappeared off the face of the earth.

It had bothered most of the folks in town, Joe running off like that. But there was nothing that anyone could prove that it hadn't happened exactly like Silas Marcum had said. Lilly knew that Marshal Woodrow had asked around, but hadn't been able to find anything.

And then Marcum had fired Charlie Gimsby, and soon all the other regular hands on the Barrel M. The men that Marcum had hired were mainly drifters and low-life that had appeared suddenly in town. Her own hands had noted that they didn't seem to actually know much about cattle, and seemed more concerned with any cowboys that accidentally drifted onto Barrel M range. They made it a point to run them off or kill them.

Lilly took another sip of brandy. Maverick was an interesting man. He talked little of his own past, something that she found fascinating. He was a man of mystery, and yet, by God he was a man. He made a woman feel safe when he was around, even if she didn't necessarily need protection.

She was a fair hand with a six-shooter, in her own right, and was downright deadly with a rifle. Her husband had made sure of it when they had come west. She had taken pleasure in seeing Ben Carew killed by Maverick. She knew in her heart that Marcum had ordered to kill her husband, much as he had probably sicked the man on Maverick. Only Maverick had been ready and expecting it where her husband had not.

Her husband had died because of it. He hadn't been expecting for Carew to ride up on him out on the range. Carew had shot him dead and claimed that her husband had been rustling cattle from the Barrel M. Her husband had been an honest man and never carried a running iron in his life. Yet, Carew had supposedly found him with one standing over a roped and tied unbranded calf.

Lilly frowned on the memory of the way the townspeople had avoided her after that. Except for Macy and Emma and, of course, her ranch hands on both of her spreads. They had gleaned the truth of the matter and stood behind her. Marshal Woodrow had as well, because her husband had been a friend to the town marshal. But his jurisdiction ended at the town line. She and her husband lived just beyond. Boulder County was one of the original seventeen counties created by the Territory of Colorado. Although Lilly and her husband had supported him, the County Sheriff Howell hadn't even bothered to ride over and investigate, despite appeals from both her and Marshal Woodrow.

Lilly hoped that Maverick could make a difference. Silas Marcum was throwing a wide loop, but she suspected that Maverick was man enough to make him reign it in. She hoped so at least. She finished her glass of brandy and headed for her bedroom. She added fuel and stoked that fire to flame before getting into her night dress and crawling into bed. She went to sleep thinking of Maverick and with a smile on her lips.

~ ~ ~

It was nigh on midnight when Jimmy returned to the mining camp. He was not surprised to find out that Major Carr was still awake. He was immediately ushered into the Major's private quarters where they were soon joined by Clyde Somersby. "Were you able to reach your former employer, Jimmy?" Carr asked.

"I was, Sir. And he is still sympathetic to our cause. He has agreed to put us up for a few days at his ranch before we head onto Old Mexico," Jimmy replied.

"Get some rest, Jimmy. We set out at dawn," Carr said, clapping him on the shoulder. Jimmy nodded wearily and headed for his bedroll.

"Are you sure that you want to do this, Major?" Clyde asked.

"As sure as I am that The South will rise again, Captain Somersby," Carr told him. "This is not an opportunity that we can afford to pass up. Except, we shall strip this ranch and the town of everything that they have to offer. What we cannot use, we shall sell in Old Mexico," Jonas Carr told him.

~ ~ ~

The night passed quickly, and Maverick was soon standing guard. The night had been a quiet one, but he was a canny enough man to know that would not last. Once Marcum heard of his plans to start ranching the range next to him, trouble would be coming hard and fast. He rolled himself a smoke and lit it. When trouble came, he would damn well meet it head on.

Chapter 19

Maverick watched the sun come up as he sipped a cup from his fresh pot of coffee. The air seemed warmer this morning, and that was a good thing. It seemed like ever since he had awakened in the carnage of that slaughtered wagon train, he had been on the run from danger. Not knowing where it might strike at him next. He wanted to put down roots, danger be damned. And that was what he was doing. Whatever dangers were in his past, he would meet them head on when the time came to face them. But for now, he was going to do what he wanted, and that was put down roots.

This ranch was going to be his point of starting over. He was going to build a new life here in Colorado. He was already a wealthy man from his part ownership in the mine with Bandy Michaels. The gold he had found in the cave on his way down from the Rockies had only increased his wealth. But Maverick wanted more than that. He wanted to ranch, to raise horses and cattle and love the land that he lived on. He was a man born to the high lonesome, at least in his current incarnation. Whoever he had been in the past; that was another lifetime. Now, he was Maverick, and that was who he would live out his days as.

He heard noises from inside the tent and soon Charlie Grimsby ambled out, stretching and groaning as he worked the kinks out of his body. Charlie was no longer a young man. He looked at Maverick. "Thank you for keeping that fire hot. It kept the tent warm," Charlie told him.

"Coffee's fresh, pour yourself a cup a'fore you start making breakfast for the men," Maverick told him.

"A cup would go down real good, for sure," Charlie told him, as he squatted next to the fire. Maverick poured him one and handed it over. Charlie held on to it to warm up his hands.

"I'm going to build something here, Charlie. Something good and that will last," Maverick said.

"I reckon you will, Maverick. You've got that look about you. You're a man who gets things done and doesn't think twice about bucking trouble. I put the word out and we'll have more help today. The old Barrel M crew that worked for Joe Morton when he owned it will ride in, ready to go to work for the Maverick brand. Not a one of them has any love for Silas Marcum," Charlie said.'

"Miss Lilly is sending some of her hands to help as well," Maverick grinned.

"She's a fine woman ... that one is. It was pretty obvious when I seen her in the café that she already sets some store by you," Charlie told him.

"I'm not sure that I am ready for that, Charlie," Maverick told him.

"Maybe not, but it's true. She's a good woman, Maverick. Don't let her get away."

"I'll have to think on that some," Maverick replied, tossing out the rest of his coffee and heading to feed the horses on the picket line as Charlie started on breakfast.

~ ~ ~

Gideon Shade and Jonathan Blocker made their way back to the saloon. The air had become warmer during the night and it was starting to melt the snow. The Chinooks winds had come, ushering in a false spring. Snow was melting quickly as they took to their beds. They had both spent the night guarding the café and the rooms in the back where Macy and Emma lived.

Maverick was out of town and they had not wanted the girls to go unprotected. The Marshal would do his best, but they both knew that it was not enough. Woodrow could handle things during the day, but even he had to sleep. They both knew that Maverick, as well as most of the townspeople set some store by those young women. Themselves included. Making sure that they were safe, well ... it was something that they were doing for not only Maverick, but for the whole town.

~ ~ ~

Colton reigned in his horse at the mining camp. It seemed odd that it would be deserted. The place was quiet, almost too quiet. He slid out of the saddle and started looking around. It didn't take long to find the dead miners. They weren't killed by injuns. He was able to read that from the tracks. Shod horses had been ridden in. Most injuns didn't shoe their horses. He stopped to study on it for a moment. Somebody had wanted it to look like an injun attack, except for the shod horses, they might well have pulled it off. Colton climbed back on his horse and headed south.

~ ~ ~

Jonas Carr and his men bypassed the town of Boulder on their way to the Barrel M ranch. Carr had felt that it would not be a good thing for men wearing the uniform of The South to be seen on the ride through the town.

Silas Marcum had welcomed them with open arms and had been more than happy to let his men rest on his ranch. Jonas Carr had followed Marcum into the house.

"How may I help you, Major?" Marcum asked.

"That is what I am hoping to find out, Mister Marcum," Carr replied.

"So, please, tell me."

"My men and I represent the surviving members of the Confederacy. I was wondering if you would be willing to contribute to our cause so that The South might yet rise again and tear victory from the ashes of defeat," Carr replied.

"I wish that I could, Major Carr. However, I find myself under attack from the Yankees, as well," Marcum responded.

"Then we will try to help you in return for giving us shelter and food to aid in the cause, Mister Marcum. How may we help you?"

"There is a Yankee calling himself Maverick that is seeking to move in on my range and he's brought in a bunch of hired gunmen to help him," Marcum said.

"Tell me more, Sir," Carr asked. Silas Marcum felt a deep sense of satisfaction knowing he had drawn the rebel major into his plan to rid himself of Maverick once and for all.

~ ~ ~

Oscar Bane had decided to stay on in Denver City. He had money wired from his accounts in St. Louis and was investing in some businesses in the boom town that had become the territorial capital. He had also invested in the railroad which was branching out from Denver to other cities and states throughout the west.

While he was currently considered well-to-do, Bane had a feeling that Denver would make him rich. Especially, if Colton was successful and put an end to Gerald Kilburn, the man currently calling himself Maverick.

It was hard to imagine that he and Kilburn had been friends once. That was back when they were boys in Boston. Kilburn was born to money though one would never know it from the way he acted. Bane hadn't come from wealth, however, and it was something that had always bothered him.

Even though they were friends, Bane had always been jealous of Kilburn's easy manner and good looks.

Girls flocked to him and rarely gave Oscar so much as a glance. Then, Katie Clinton, a girl that Oscar had pursued relentlessly since grade school had accepted Kilburn's offer of marriage. That was it for Bane, his resentment turned into a full-blown hatred of Gerald Kilburn.

When the war broke out, Kilburn had enlisted to fight for the Union. After he had left Boston, Bane broke into the house where Kilburn and Katie had moved after their marriage. He had viciously raped her and slit her throat so that she could never tell anyone and set fire to the house. Later, when he heard that Kilburn had sworn vengeance on the man that had murdered his wife, Bane had hired Colton to find the man and kill him. Bane had left Boston and headed for St. Louis. That way, if Kilburn lived and returned to Boston, he would no longer be there.

But Colton and the Johnny Rebs had both failed to kill Gerald Kilburn who had quickly risen in rank to that of a colonel in the Union Army. The war ended, and Kilburn had returned to Boston, but became wary of the multiple attempts on his life. He had sold off his properties and many business interests and headed west with a wagon train. Bane's spies sent word of the wagon train's route and he sent men to wipe it out, but somehow, Kilburn had once more eluded death at his hands. It was infuriating. Bane wanted terribly to lash out, but he knew that would accomplish nothing. No, it would be better to wait and let Colton deal with it.

~ ~ ~

Lilly Cambridge was wearing a stylish split gaucho skirt that would allow her to sit in her saddle astride easier and high leather western boots. She accompanied that with a warm wool shirt circled at the waist with a wide leather belt and polished silver buckle and a short leather jacket. She would have preferred a pair of jeans, but her mother had raised her to be as lady-like as possible. And she at least tried to present herself in this fashion for others, like Macy and Emma. She knew that both of the young women looked up to her.

She stopped at the café to pick up the large picnic basket that she had dropped off earlier. She wanted to surprise Maverick and the men with some of the café's best dishes. Macy had looked her over and nodded her approval, a twinkle in her eye. Bull Satterly was waiting outside. He was riding with her in case of trouble. Bull was a top hand and she trusted him with her life. Bull looked at the large basket she was carrying and climbed down to help her rig it to her saddle.

"I got one question, Ma'am," Bull said, after he was back on his horse.

"What's that, Bull?" Lilly asked.

"Do we get a taste of them vittles, as well? Charlie Grimsby is a good cook and all, but he don't hold a candle to them two gals that run the café," Bull said.

"Yes, Bull, there is enough for us, too. Now, let's get going!"

~ ~ ~

Over at Maverick's spread, a corral and lean-to to hold the horses and protect them from weather was already up and logs to form the walls were being notched and gotten ready to be set into place on the foundation. Maverick and Hank were spreading wet mud on the top of the foundation to settle the first logs on. By resting the logs on the thick slabs of mud, it would help block out wind from entering the cabin at floor level. The first logs were set in place lengthwise, and then they built the mud shelf on the foundation stones at the end and had those set in place. A couple of boys pounded the logs down into notches to lock them tight.

The boys had surprised him by cutting floor boards so Maverick and Luke had built staggered walls along the bottom of the foundation and the boards were set in place. Once the cabin was done, a hatch would be cut into the crawlspace and an escape tunnel would be dug that would come out under where the barn would be built. When the floor was in place, the rest of the logs went up to form the walls. More boards were cut to make an a-frame roof. The tent had been struck once they had started work for the day. About noon, Maverick called a break for lunch. He was just washing up in the creek when Lilly and Bull rode in. Maverick dried his hands and arms and walked over to greet her.

"Miss Lilly, nice of you to drop by, and your beauty is a sight for sore eyes, but I'm not quite set up to receive visitors yet," Maverick greeted her. Not that she needed it, he reached up to help her down encircling her small waist with his large gruff hands. Lilly slid off her horse and Bull got down and untied the basket.

"I come bearing gifts, Maverick," Lilly smiled at him, blushing and Maverick felt his knees go a little week.

"Now what the heck is going on out here? I ain't got lunch ready yet," Charlie said, as he walked out of his cook's tent.

"That's okay, Charlie," Lilly told him. "Miss Emma and Miss Macy sent some of the café's best dishes for the whole crew, and they sent you a couple of blueberry pies." Charlie stood for a moment, licking his lips.

"Did you say blueberry pies?" he asked.

"I did. Emma said that you gave her the recipe and she hopes that it tastes as good as one of yours."

"Well now, I'll certainly need to taste it to find out." He looked at Maverick.

"What are you waiting on, call the boys in to eat," Charlie said.

The hands had been working hard and had built up their appetites. They made short work of the food in the basket and then what Charlie had prepared for their lunch, as well.

"Lilly, thank you for coming out," Maverick told her after enjoying the meal.

"I wanted to see you," Lilly said, unabashedly.

"I'm glad. I was missing you," Maverick told her, his arms slipping around her tiny frame as he pulled her to him and kissed her hard. They were out of sight of the men, so they let themselves surrender to the moment. They were both breathing hard when the kiss ended.

"I hope that means that you'll be coming to call soon," Lilly said, breathlessly.

"Count on it," Maverick told her, meaning every word. Finally, she and Bull mounted up and headed back to town and the men went back to work. That night, everyone slept inside a warm cabin.

Chapter 20

The sun was shining bright and the air was warming up. A light mist hung over the snow on the ground as Colton rode into town. He headed for the saloon first. Whiskey sounded good after his time on the trail from Denver to Boulder. It would help drive the chill from his bones after riding the wintry trail.

There were just a few people in the saloon when Colton entered. He walked straight to the bar. The big man behind the bar approached him, looking him over. "What can I get for you?" the man asked.

"Whiskey please, and leave the bottle. It's been a damn cold ride."

"Yes, Sir. Where you ride in from?" the barkeeper asked as he grabbed a bottle from beneath the shelf and opened it to pour a shot. He recapped the bottle and sat it on the bar next to the shot glass.

"Denver. I wasn't too prepared for that storm," Colton said, as he slid two dollars across the bar.

"I imagine not. They come along every now and then, it is winter, after all," Jonathan Blocker answered sarcastically.

Gideon Shade was watching it all from across the room. He shuffled the cards in his hands without even thinking about it. He had recognized the man. He had met Roger Colton before. He was also aware of the man's reputation as a fast gun and as a man with little or no scruples. Roger Colton was a killer for hire. It seemed awful funny, him showing up here so soon after Maverick. It was something for Shade to think about and study on.

~ ~ ~

Hiram King, Marcum's main foreman, frowned as he looked down at the clearing. A house had gone up as well as a corral and lean-to. There was sign of other structures being built up as well. The boss was not going to be happy about that. Yet, there was little that Hiram could do on his own. Not with that salty bunch of hands that Maverick had working for him. Hiram knew many of them first hand and knew that their reputations had been earned. Personally, he didn't see the problem with these neighbors, but Mister Marcum wanted them gone. He shook his head and started back towards the Barrel M to deliver the news about Maverick and his men. It was not something that he was looking forward to.

~ ~ ~

Jonas Carr sipped at the brandy that Silas Marcum had provided him with. He had listened to Marcum's tale of woe, of being manhandled by a no-account cowboy that had sucker punched him and then beat him without giving him a chance to recover. A drifter who had then had the audacity to get the bank to loan him money to buy up the range bordering his own. Carr had perked up at the mention of the bank. Carr made sympathetic noises in all of the right places and then turned the conversation to the town and the bank, learning everything that he could. Jonas Carr was making his own plans for the town of Boulder and leaving Silas Marcum holding the bag and the blame.

~ ~ ~

The warm weather had remained and the men working for Maverick made the best of it. The house, cook shack, and bunkhouse were done, and the barn was getting damn close. Maverick had ridden into town and brought back a wagon full of supplies, one of which was an iron cook stove for Charlie and a couple of wood burning stove for the bunkhouse. After all, there would be a lot of men to feed. The fireplace that he had built was quite adequate for warming his quarters. He had, also stocked Charlie's larder to the fullest so that the meals were excellent. He had bought some cows from Lilly Cambridge to start his herd, and had sent a wire to a man down in Texas that was willing to drive more cattle up to him. The rest of the cattle would arrive in late spring.

Saturday had arrived, and the men had done a fair piece of work through the week, and Maverick had allowed some of the men go into town, but not all of them. He made them draw straws to see who would go and who would stay to guard the ranch. Luke Cantrell was happy to have been selected to go to town. He had been pining over Miss Emma something awful.

Maverick rode in with the bunch which included a couple of the men that Luke had hired as well as some of the men that had worked for Joe Morton on the Barrel M before Marcum had bought the place. Maverick had taken time to get to know each of the men that he had hired, and he knew them all to be good hands, everyone a man to ride the river with. That was one of the highest compliments that a western man could pay to another. They all had grit and he knew that he couldn't have asked for a better crew. He had left Charlie Grimsby in charge, because he knew that everyone at the ranch liked and respected Charlie. They would follow his orders.

The cattle were bunched in the lowlands and a couple of the boys were keeping an eye on them. According to the testimony of stockmen in this region, the coming warm winds of the Chinook is a critical period and often the means of saving their herds not only from starvation but from freezing. Instinctively, the cattle seem to anticipate its coming, and may be seen standing knee-deep in the snow with their heads turned toward the mountains, anxiously awaiting the arrival of relief

Maverick knew that the warm spell wouldn't last. The Chinooks came in late February, but didn't last more than a couple of weeks, and then the winter returned with a vengeance. He planned to make the most of the warm weather while he could. Were it not for the visitations of this warm, dry wind the vast stock ranges would have to be abandoned in the winter, as the cattle and other stock, prevented by the snow from securing access to the nutritious grasses on the plains, would not be able to secure nourishment sufficient to sustain life.

Maverick wanted to see Lilly Cambridge while in town as much as Luke wanted to see Miss Emma. Lilly had been in his thoughts a lot over the past week. Her beauty was unparalleled, and her heart was pure. She was a good woman. A woman of character and grace but, by God, one could sense she was a tough one. A woman not to be challenged.

When they reached Boulder, Luke headed straight for the café as expected, but Maverick took his time and headed for the saloon. He wanted to check in with Jonathan Blocker and Gideon Shade. He figured that they had been keeping an eye out on any strangers that had come to town as well as watching over the girls that ran the café. Maverick walked in after stomping mud off of his boots. He walked to the bar and had Jonathan draw him a draft of beer before walking over to the empty table where Shade was playing solitaire.

"Maverick," Shade acknowledged him, as he sat down.

"How have things been, Gideon?" Maverick asked.

"Fairly quiet, except for a gunman that rode in," Shade replied, flipping the cards onto the table. He found one he could use and transferred it to one of the row of cards.

"Know anything about him?" Maverick asked.

"Fella by the name of Roger Colton. He's a hand with a gun, saw him in a shootout down around Amarillo," Shade replied.

"He mention why he's in town?"

"Said that he's looking for a fellow he knew in the war," Shade shrugged.

"Interesting," Maverick allowed.

"That's what I thought," Shade nodded. "I kind of got the feeling that he might be looking for you."

"Why is that?" Maverick asked.

"Just a feeling. You said yourself, you don't remember your past," Shade prodded him.

"True enough. Describe him to me," Maverick requested. Shade did just that and Maverick filed the description away. The man did sound familiar, but he couldn't quite remember. Maybe it would come to him later.

"Does Marshal Woodrow know that he's in town?"

"He does. Marshal had a talk with him, told him if he used his gun in Boulder that he's be arrested unless there were at least half a dozen witnesses to side with him," Shade replied.

"I'm going to go talk to Woodrow and see if there are any dodgers out on this Colton guy. Thanks for the report," Maverick told him. He stood and headed out the door. Gideon watched him go.

The streets of Boulder were more mud and slush than anything with the snowmelt. Maverick stomped as much mud off his boots as he could before entering the marshal's office. Woodrow was at his desk, reading glasses perched on his nose, as he was working his way through the stack of wanted posters.

"Looking for Roger Colton in there?" Maverick asked.

"How did you know?" Woodrow looked up at him.

"Gideon Shade told me about him riding in."

"Nice of him, he ain't in there," Woodrow frowned, as he shoved the stack aside.

"Meaning you've no excuse to have him move along out of town," Maverick said. It wasn't a question.

"Not one. I did tell him if he used his guns, he would be arrested and held until the Colorado Territory County Sheriff rode in to collect him," Woodrow replied.

"Don't try it unless you have the drop on him. From what Gideon Shade said, he's mighty sudden with his gun."

"Maverick, I can't let that stop me, or I'll have to hang up my badge, and then where will the townspeople be?"

"They'd be better off with you alive than with you dead, Marshal. If you need to go after him and I'm not in town, take Gideon Shade with you. Shade has seen him work and knows what to look for. It'll give you a better chance at living to tell the tale."

"I appreciate that, Maverick. I truly do. You got any other suggestions to improve on my health and well-being?" Woodrow asked, humorously.

"None that I can think of right off hand," Maverick grinned at him.

"Thank God for small favors," Woodrow rolled his eyes.

~ ~ ~

Lilly Cambridge was waiting in the café when Maverick walked in. Macy made a bee-line for their table with the coffee pot and filled his cup right away. "What can I get for you Mister Maverick?" she asked.

"Hello, Miss Macy. Bring me a steak and potatoes and some biscuits, please," Maverick told her. Macy headed for the kitchen. He looked over at Miss Lilly with a pleased look on his face.

"It's so nice to see you, Miss Lilly, I have missed you," he smiled, and for once it reached his eyes. He reached for her slender hand.

"It's good to see you too, Maverick, I have thought a lot about you," Lilly smiled back at his as she cupped his cold fingers.

"Thank you for sending your men to help. We've got the headquarters built. I've sent word to Texas to buy a bunch of heads from the Lazy T. They will be bringing cattle in the spring to build my herd."

"I'm glad to hear it. Do you think you can hold out against Marcum that long?" Lilly asked.

"If I need to. The man is a bully, Lilly. I hate bullies with a passion," Maverick replied.

"I could tell that about you," Lilly said, as she sipped at her coffee.

"I aim to break Silas Marcum and run him out of the country."

"How do you plan to do that?"

"I'm going to expose the son of a bitch for what he is, forgive my foul mouth. I don't usually speak such in front of a fine lady as you. Once people know about him, he won't have any allies at all in the area."

"You seem sure of that."

"I am. Silas Marcum is a bully. He's used to getting his way. I don't aim to let that happen here," Maverick said.

"I'm glad to hear it. Nobody, except maybe the banker, likes him, and I am not too sure about the banker," Lilly said.

"I have it on good authority that he doesn't," Maverick told her.

"There is a stranger in town. He keeps pretty much to himself," Lilly told him.

"A gunslinger by the name of Roger Colton. I already heard about him," Maverick said.

"Do you know why he's here?"

"I think that he may be looking for me."

"Maverick, why is that?" She squeezed his hand harder.

"I can't remember, Lilly. I wish I could, but I can't."

"That has to be hard."

"It is, Sweetheart."

"So, what are you going to do about it?"

"Honestly, I'm not sure yet," Maverick said.

At that point, Macy reappeared with his steak and potatoes and Maverick ate his meal with Lilly at his side. She had eaten earlier and chose to just sit with him during his dinner. He missed the winks that passed between Macy and Lilly Cambridge. He had no idea how close he was to going over the edge with the beautiful Miss Lilly Cambridge. He thought to himself that it might not be so bad to be hog-tied and branded by her.

~ ~ ~

Roger Colton had moved on from Blocker's to a smaller saloon called 'The Rusty Bucket'. It catered more to men of his ilk. He spent a lot of time nursing a beer as he listened to the town gossip. Maverick had made a name for himself when he had faced down Silas Marcum and tossed him ass over tea kettle into the muddy street. According to the talk that Colton had picked up, Maverick had made himself a dangerous enemy. He had already decided to ride out to see Silas Marcum.

Chapter 21

Roger Colton had been inside the Boulder General Store when Maverick and his men rode into town. He had been busy buying supplies for his saddle bags because he knew that once he had killed the man he knew as Gerald Kilburn, he would have to light a shuck out of the state in a hurry. He had known men like Marshal Woodrow before, and given reason enough, the marshal wasn't the kind to let a thing like jurisdiction slow him down or stop him.

Woodrow had been a lawman for a couple of decades, and he hadn't gotten to be as old as he was by being foolish. He had built his reputation by working as a law dog in tough cattle towns where drives ended up and range wars began. There was no way that Colton was believing that Woodrow had taken the job in Boulder because he had in anyway slowed down.

No, the Marshal was a shrewd and knowing sort of man and he knew Colton by reputation. Knew what kind of man he was and what he probably intended to do. The only thing the Marshal didn't know was the identity of his target. However, it played out, Colton would have to be right careful if he wanted to get away with his hide intact.

His prime purchases were more ammunition for both his Colt and his Winchester, makings for a smoke, coffee, some jerky and some bacon and hardtack. All of which would come in useful on the trail once his work here was done. Maybe he'd drift on up towards Wyoming or thereabouts. He'd heard the town of Laramie offered many opportunities.

~ ~ ~

Hiram King was mighty uncomfortable after delivering the news to Silas Marcum that Maverick had already built a house and corral on the range next to the Barrel M spread. Hiram had been promoted to *Segundo* after the death of Ben Carew at the hands of the man called Maverick. Unlike Carew, King was a cattleman and not a warrior. Sure, he'd ride for the brand, but if he felt something was wrong, he felt duty bound to point it out. Except that wasn't the kind of man that Marcum wanted running his ranch for him.

"Hiram, I want you to take some of the boys and ride over and raze that new cabin to the ground! I want it done tonight!" Silas Marcum roared.

"I cain't do it, Boss. Maverick bought the property fair and square. He owns it all nice and legal. I'm not ashamed to say I won't be part of breaking the law." Hiram stood up to Marcum, wondering if he was about to die.

"Then get out now, Hiram, a'fore I kill ya'. I won't have a man on my spread who isn't going to follow my orders!" Marcum snarled at him.

"I reckon I'll be on my way then," Hiram said stiffly, backing out of the room.

There were a lot of hands on the Barrel M that he didn't trust any farther than a tooth-sore rattlesnake. Once he was outside of the house, Hiram forked his horse and headed away from the Barrel M. He knew where he was a going too. He wasn't about to let them ol' boys on the Maverick Ranch be caught by surprise. He hoped that he was doing the right thing. Marcum had seemed even crazier since that Rebel Major Carr and his men that had ridden in.

~ ~ ~

"The audacity of that man, Mister Marcum," Jonas Carr said, with a tight smile. His lips were curled around a cigar that he was smoking.

"I need a *Segundo* I can trust. Apparently, Hiram King wasn't that man," Silas Marcum spat disgustedly.

"If you like, I can send a few of my men with yours to raid this upstart's ranch," Carr told him.

"I'd appreciate that, Major, as sort of a payment for me lettin' you men bunk down here on my property. I truly would," Marcum replied.

"Have your men ready to ride at dawn," Carr said.

~ ~ ~

Gideon Shade had left Blocker's Saloon and made his way down the street to the Rusty Bucket. He wanted to check up on that no count Roger Colton and see what the man was up to. He liked Maverick, even if he wasn't completely sure that the man really had no memory of his past. But this fella' Roger Colton was a stone-cold killer. Shade knew that there was no way he could let Maverick face Colton alone. If that meant that he had to step in, then he would. Maverick hadn't disrespected him when they had met in the Jonathan's bar. He had just accepted Shade as another solitary traveler moving through the west.

'The Rusty Bucket' was busy, but that was not really unusual for a Saturday night. 'The Bucket', as it was known was a hangout for low-life's and criminals of every stripe. For the most part, they kept their heads down and stayed clear of Marshal Woodrow when he came around. Shade walked in and made his way to one of the poker tables. He bought into the game and seated himself where he could keep an eye on Roger Colton.

~ ~ ~

Maverick had walked Miss Lilly home to her boarding house and then had mounted up and headed back to the ranch. He trusted the men that he had brought to town not to get into trouble that they couldn't get out of by using their heads. He preferred a thinking crew because they were smart enough not to let themselves get drawn into trouble or get too much in the bottle.

As much as he had enjoyed this trip to town and Miss Lilly's company, it felt good to be by himself as he rode through the night. This felt the best of him as he rode the high trails, enjoying the cool evening air and the sight of the night sky.

The stars looked like diamonds on a blue-black velvet blanket. It was at times like this, that the man who called himself Maverick felt most alive. He had been born to the high lonesome. He could feel it in his bones. And yet, he had chosen to settle and put down roots. Would the wanderlust claim him again? Or was he finally done with that life? It was a question to consider. But not tonight.

Tonight, he wanted to just be one under the stars and to ride the wild and wooly high lonesome. It was something that he needed as much as he needed to breathe the cool air itself. It took him less than an hour to reach the ranch from town, and he was surprised to see that lanterns still burned in the house.

He put his horse in the corral and made his way to the main house. Hank met him in the doorway. "Wasn't expecting you back yet, Boss, but to tell the truth, I'm glad you're here," Hank told him.

"I didn't see the need to spend the night in town, Hank. Now what's going on?" Maverick asked.

"Come on into the kitchen," Hank said. He headed deeper into the large log house with Maverick on his heels.

"What's going on, Hank?" Maverick asked.

"Best you hear it for yourself and decide," Hank said, as they entered the kitchen. A man was sitting at the table that Maverick didn't recognize, but it was obvious that Hank knew him. The man rose as Maverick entered the warm kitchen.

"Hiram, this here's the Boss. You repeat to him what you just told me."

"Mister Maverick, my name is Hiram King, pleased to meet you, Sir. I'd replaced Ben Carew when he was killed as *Segundo* over at the Barrel M, that is til' tonight when I was given my walking papers," King explained.

"And why was that, Mister King?" Maverick asked, coolly.

"I was ordered to come and raze this place, burn it to the ground by Mister Marcum. He still bears a lot of ill will towards you for what happened at the café," Hiram said.

"You figure that Marcum's boys will hit tonight?"

"Not just his boys, he done took up with some Johnny Reb Major and his outfit, a fella goes by the name of Carr." Maverick's head snapped up.

"Major Jonas Carr?" Maverick demanded.

"Yes, Sir!"

"You recognize the name, Boss?" Hank asked.

"Major Jonas Carr was a guerilla leader, a savage killer who rode for the gray, but not out of patriotism. He and his men were nothing more than mad-dog killers. I chased him and his men all over the south in the war," Maverick said, his eyes wide with shock. He was starting to remember. Remember who he was and why he had been running. He looked at Hank.

"Send Fred Tuttle to get the boys back here pronto. We'll need them before dawn."

"I'll go wake him up and get him moving," Hank said, walking out of the room. Maverick looked at Hiram King.

"Are you willing to stand against Marcum and tell this story to Marshal Woodrow?" Maverick asked.

"I am," King said. "I only hired on with Marcum because I was riding the grub line and desperate for work."

"I'll pay you forty dollars a month and found if you are willing to ride for my brand," Maverick told him.

"I'm willing as long as I don't have to break the law," King nodded.

"Hiram, I'm an honest man, tough but honest. I'd never ask that of any of my men."

"I believe you, Mister Maverick."

"Good. Find a spot and take a rest. I'll rouse you and the boys before the attack comes."

"Thanks, Boss. I'm right tired," King replied. He stood and looked for a spot to lay down.

Maverick returned to the kitchen table and poured himself a cup of coffee. His memory was coming back, and it was coming back fast. His name was Gerald Kilburn, and he had been a Colonel in the Union Army. He had been tasked with finding and arresting Jonas Carr.

A few months after he had been given his commission, his wife had been raped and murdered back in Boston while he was away from home. The news had shocked him. Then, he was shot in Charleston and left for dead. He had thought at the time that Jonas Carr was behind it. He had headed back home once the war was over. Carr and his men had gone underground, and Kilburn had wanted to look more closely into the rape and murder of his wife.

Men had been waiting for him in Boston and he had barely escaped with his life. They had been waiting at Pittsburg and again in Louisville. Kilburn had managed to escape each time, but it had taken everything he had to do so. He had joined the wagon train in St. Louis, but once again, men had come. They thought they had killed him that time too, but they had just stolen his memory. But now ... it was back.

He was remembering things, more and more events, days, months, years that he had thought had been lost forever. He thought about his childhood friend, Oscar. Oscar had always been sweet on his wife, since their early school years together and had attended their wedding. Could he be behind her murder? It just couldn't be but it was certainly something for him to consider.

~ ~ ~

None of the boys were happy about being rousted in the middle of the night, but when they heard why they had been ordered to return to the ranch, they all were in a hurry to get back to their boss man. None of them wanted to miss out on a fight and would protect Maverick. He had been very good to his men and they wouldn't forget that.

Luke's only regret was that he hadn't been able to tell Emma goodbye before he had left. But he had no desire to be left out of the fight and show his allegiance to Maverick. He hated Silas Marcum, hated him with all his heart.

~ ~ ~

Jonas Carr had taken charge of the men that Marcum had lent him to hit the Maverick ranch. Silas Marcum had no idea that Carr planned to set him up for the murder of this man called Maverick and for the robbery of 'The Boulder Bank.' They had spent a couple of hours infiltrating the area around the Maverick spread in the darkness. He planned to strike at dawn. Once this Maverick and his men were dead, it would be easy enough to pin the deaths on Marcum, especially if a couple of Maverick's men were found dead on the Silas Marcum spread as if it were a range war. And if a couple of the Marcum men were discovered dead at the bank, so much the better for pointing the finger at Marcum. Carr smiled. It was a good plan.

~ ~ ~

Gideon Shade kept an eye on Roger Colton until he retired to the hotel in town for the night. Once Colton was bedded down, he returned to Blocker's Saloon. Jonathan Blocker had given him a key and he let himself inside. He was sure that Jonathan was over at the café keeping an eye on Miss Macy and Miss Emma while the young girls slept upstairs above their establishment, as he closed his eyes and drifted off to sleep. Shade hoped that he was wrong, that Colton would leave the two young women alone. But if he didn't, Shade was more than ready to face Colton in the street.

Gideon knew that he could beat the man to the draw if it came to that, even though he hoped that it would not. It had been a while since he had been called upon to use his gun, but he knew that he had not lost his edge. He spent many hours practicing firing his weapon out on the range.

Gideon wished that he could talk to Blocker, but Jonathan was a hard man to wake up once he had gone to sleep. That meant that Gideon would be out on the street in the morning and doing the best he could to keep Macy and Emma safe.

Chapter 22

The first lightening of the sky indicating that dawn wasn't too far away was just starting to become visible. Maverick and his men were set up and ready, as was his new hire, Hiram King. Some of the men were stationed in the woods surrounding the clearing, well-hidden and waiting for Silas Marcum and Jonas Carr to make their move. All of their guns were loaded, and each man had plenty of extra shells. Maverick had a few sticks of dynamite handy as well.

He wasn't going to accept Major Jonas Carr to escape again. No, he planned to kill the Confederate guerilla leader once and for all. Hank was the only man in Maverick's employ that knew he had regained his memory and he had asked the man not to mention it. Not until he had figured out who was trying to kill him. There was just too much trouble dogging Gerald Kilburn's trail. So, it might just be better for him to remain as Maverick.

He hadn't invited the trouble that seemed to follow him, but it sure had a way of plaguing him no matter where he went. He had grown accustomed to the fact since he had awakened in the remains of that slaughtered wagon train. But, Maverick had grown weary of the turmoil and the constant watching over his back.

Jonas Carr had put Marcum's men in the first wave of raiders to ride in on the Maverick spread. Marcum had insisted on leading his men in their charge, which was fine with Carr. He had planned all along on Marcum being killed. He didn't want to leave and witnesses behind. Once Marcum was dead, and Carr had no doubt that the man would die in the attack on this Maverick's ranch, Carr and his men would attack and wipe the town of Boulder off the face of the earth before they looted the bank and headed south to Old Mexico.

Carr had been a master strategist during the war. He expected to catch Maverick and his men in the main house and surprise them. They wouldn't be expecting an attack this early in the day, if at all. Marcum's men would be carrying lit torches that would make them easy to see for the defenders and thus more likely to catch a bullet. But they were likely to set the buildings ablaze. He and his men would take the horses from the corral and then kill any of Marcum's men that survived.

Maverick spotted the first torch several minutes before the man carrying it was close enough to attack. He smiled as he cocked his Winchester rifle and took aim. He fired at the torch and was rewarded with a scream as the man fell to the ground. Then more torches appeared, and his men opened fire.

The first wave of raiders crashed to the ground, bleeding from deadly accurate fire. Then, Carr and his men attacked. So far, the men that Maverick had had positioned in the trees had not opened fire. As the rebel contingent rode in, they started shooting.

Maverick lit a bundle of dynamite and tossed it into the attacking force. It exploded, knocking men out of the saddle and into the path of withering gunfire. Soon, the attack was over. None of the attacking force had survived. Maverick was able to identify Marcum and Jonas Carr, though Carr's body was blown in half by the exploding dynamite. There was no remorse and Maverick still felt a strong sense of personal satisfaction at the man's death.

~ ~ ~

Jonathan Blocker was weary when he returned to his saloon from his watch at Miss Emma's and he quickly tumbled into bed. He hadn't bothered talking to Gideon before going to sleep. He just hoped that everything would be over soon.

~ ~ ~

Gideon Shade was up with the dawn. Blocker had already gone to bed, so Gideon didn't bother him. He knew that the man would be awake in four hours to open the saloon. Shade stepped out onto the street and headed for 'Miss Emma's Café,' It would be opening soon, and he planned to be among its first customers when it did. He was in the mood for some biscuits and gravy.

Shade could see the lights on in the back of the café, but he sat on a bench on the boardwalk across the street as the sun started to climb into the sky. So far, he was the only person out on the streets, but he knew that wouldn't last.

After a bit, Macy unlocked the door of the café and turned the open sign around to face the street. Gideon stood and crossed the street to be the first customer of the day. Macy brought him coffee and a pretty smile. "What can I get you this morning, Mister Shade?" she asked.

"Steak and eggs to start with, please. A man needs a good meal to start his day," Shade told her. Macy carried his order to the back just as Marshal Woodrow walked in. He walked over and took the seat next to Shade. Neither man spoke of the fact that they both had a wall at their backs. They understood and knew that it wasn't necessary.

"Marshal."

"Shade. I take it Blocker's getting some sleep?" Woodrow asked.

"You'd be right."

"Figured that, after I noticed him keeping an eye on this place all night and then you coming out to take over for him before dawn."

"Well, we kind of promised Maverick that we'd look after the girls until he settles things with Silas Marcum."

"I appreciate it too. The whole town sets store by Macy and Emma and would hate to see anything happen to them, and I can't watch them all the time," Woodrow said. Macy appeared with a cup and filled it with hot black coffee. Woodrow thanked her and ordered eggs and toast. The café was starting to fill up with the breakfast crowd.

"Is Colton still hanging around?" Shade asked.

"Well, he ain't moved along just yet. Seems to me like he's waiting on something."

"Like Maverick riding back into town?"

"Maybe. In that case, he won't have long to wait."

"Why's that?"

"Here comes Maverick now," Woodrow said.

~ ~ ~

Roger Colton spotted the man riding into town. He recognized Gerald Kilburn instantly, no matter what name he was using. Kilburn was his only failure and he aimed to rectify that now. The last time had been a long distance shot with a rifle. He wouldn't make that mistake again. No, this time he would meet him face to face and kill the son of a bitch once and for all. Then he would go collect from Oscar Bane.

He watched as Maverick climbed off his horse and tied it to the rail. Colton stepped down off the boardwalk and into the muddy street. He started walking towards Kilburn. So far, Kilburn hadn't noticed him yet, but that was about to change. "Kilburn, turn and face me!" Colton yelled. Kilburn stepped down off the boardwalk and walked to the middle of the street.

"Do I know you?" Kilburn asked.

"I missed you in Charleston," Colton called.

"You didn't miss. You got a name?"

"Colton."

"You going to talk me to death or what?" Maverick asked. Colton grabbed for his gun. It hadn't even cleared leather when he felt something strike him in the chest and he stumbled backward before falling into the mud. Coolly, Maverick punched the two spent shells from his gun and reloaded it before slipping it back into its holster.

~ ~ ~

"Marshal," Maverick said, as Woodrow and Shade charged out of the café.

"I've never seen anybody draw that fast, Maverick, and I've seen Hardin and a number of other gunmen over the years," Woodrow said.

"Colton's been chasing me across the country since the war ended. He won't be chasing me anymore," Maverick replied.

"You recognized him?" Gideon Shade asked, somewhat dumbfounded.

"My memory came back. Silas Marcum and a rebel major named Jonas Carr attacked my ranch this morning, they were going to kill us all and burn it to the ground but my boys took care of them, took care of them all. I spent the last couple years of the war chasing Carr and his guerillas. As soon as I heard his name, everything came back."

"Maverick, are you all right, Darling?" Lilly Cambridge gasped, as she ran up to the men. She'd heard the shots and the commotion from her room at the boarding house and ran down the stairs and into the street as fast as she could, her long bed gowns flowing behind her, her red hair unpinned tumbled around and framed her beautiful face. Maverick took her into his strong arms.

"Sweetheart, I'm fine, Lilly. A lot has happened, and I'd rather tell it over hot coffee and breakfast. Will you join me?" He asked, as he gazed into her eyes.

"I'd love to," Lilly smiled up at him, glad to know that he hadn't been harmed.

~ ~ ~

"So, what are you going to do, now that you know who you are?" Lilly asked him, after she's been told the whole story, as they sat closely at the dining table. Maverick leaned back in his chair.

"I've been thinking about that some. As far as anybody knows, Gerry Kilburn is dead. I think I want to keep it that way. I came west to make a fresh start. Maverick seems as good a name as any to make it with.

"Is there a missus in your future?" Lilly asked, smiled teasingly into his eyes.

"I believe there might be," Maverick smiled, as he gazed back at her.

Thank you for reading.

Please review this book. Reviews help others find Absolutely Amazing eBooks and inspire us to keep providing these marvelous tales.

If you would like to be put on our email list to receive updates on new releases, contests, and promotions, please go to AbsolutelyAmazingEbooks.com and sign up.

About the Author

Bill Craig is the best-selling author of more than 60 novels spread across the genres from mystery to pulp to science fiction to westerns. Bill is best know for his Marlow Key West mysteries and his Mitch Cooper mysteries. Bill often likes to say that it only took him 34 years to become an overnight success.

ABSOLUTELY AMAZING eBOOKS

AbsolutelyAmazingEbooks.com
or AA-eBooks.com